THE FACELESS WOMAN
THE OBSIDIAN SPINDLE SAGA
BOOK NINE

RUSSELL NOHELTY

SPECIAL THANKS

Talinda Willard, HyliaKumatora, Chris Roeszler, Amy Teegan, Chip Orlikowski, RHR, Victoria Nohelty, Alexander Joyner, Pierino Gattei, Caspar Williams, Gerald P. McDaniel, Walter Weiss, Sunny Side Up, Kenny Endlich, Amber Reeves, Joshua Bowers, Elias Rosner, Noah Carruba, John "AcesofDeath7" Mullens, Jamie Minnich, Rowan Stone, Taiga Char, BAOCHAU TRAN, Jeff Lewis, Dave Baxter, Chad Bowden, David Irgang, James Kralik, Emerson Kasak, Matthew Johnson, Paul Rose Jr., Shannon, Dr. Charles Elbert Norton III, Edward Nycz Jr., Jessica Meuth, Caledonia, GMarkC, Chris Cheek, Bianca Tatjana Višić Ritorto, John Otway Jr, Brett Bennett, Jason 'XenoPhage' Frisvold, Scott Chisholm, Amanda Sarah, Alexandra Corrsin, Giles Fox, Rick Parker, H, Rob Steinberger, Alec Loases, David Stephenson, Anthony James Frandsen, JohnDoe, Joshua Easter, MadCatter (Cat Fleming), Kevin Potter, Bill Lisse, Michael Szewczyk, Robert Woods Tienken, Ronald L Weston, Karen Haughn, Shem Bingman, Susan Wilson, Brigitte Ziegler, Matt Soucy, Alyssa, Michelle Pelo, Richard A Shirley, PerryC, Elizabeth Kiefer, Tim, Nicolas Mandujano

III, Karen Roads, Rhel ná DecVandé, Zeb Berryman, Al Gonzalez, S. D., Jörn Flath, Rick Radzville, Aaron Loren, Justise Briones(That/Them), Genevieve Slunka, Michael DeCarlo, Kitty Crab, Jeanne L. Warner, Vi Ta, Bridget D Laurent, Jaime Bialer, Wendy Martinez, Nicholas Harezga, Mira Hunter, Cara Reasner, Lori Case, Melevorn, Rebecca Hill, Jane R., Talia Denham, Jordan Harju, Jesse Coe, Greg Levick, and Andrew Messiah.

CHAPTER I

ROSE

"And would you say these fairies are dangerous?"

"Of course not," I replied. The lights of the TV studio beat down on me, flushing my already rosy cheeks. Sweat would have beaded on my face if I hadn't been caked in three inches of powdered makeup. "Not any more dangerous than anything else in the world, that is."

Three months earlier, the sky opened over a small mountain pass in Switzerland, and I led an army of fairies in a final battle against the wicked witch, Nimue, banishing her from Earth. We were victorious, but in my eagerness to defeat the evil queen, I had failed to think about the fact that every satellite across the world from the Russians to the United States to Google would get a front row seat to conclusive proof about the existence of magic, something faekind had worked hard to keep secret for thousands of years, even going so far as to burning the Library of Alexandria so they could fade into the myth and memory.

Trevor, the pompadoured news anchor, had been grilling me with questions for five minutes, as if I hadn't answered every one of them a hundred times before. "But they have magic, and if the Battle of the Obsidian Spindle told us anything, it's that magic can be quite destructive in the wrong hands."

Camera crews from all over the world had raced to the scene, but the battle was over soon after it began. Only one crew from the tiny town of Crezvark that was tucked into the base of the mountain managed to get any footage, and they were savvy enough to sell it to every news organization in the world, causing frenzy and outrage across every country on Earth.

"But in the right hands, magic can be beautiful," I said with as much positive energy as I could muster after my third interview in as many hours. "Nimue was—is a horrible person, but I've met so many wonderful magical beings over the last few years who used their powers for good. Their powers can heal the sick, rebuild cities, and extend life."

"Or they can destroy it. Isn't that just as true?"

I had made the rounds on every new station on four continents since I became the de facto spokesperson for the entirety of magical kind. I begged them to talk to somebody else, but I was a reasonably attractive, young, white woman, who fit their delicate sensibilities, which made me the perfect person to put on camera.

"You're focusing on the wrong thing," I huffed. "Everything has both an upside and a downside. Nuclear power can help end our dependence on fossil fuels that are killing the environment, but it is incredibly toxic and can be harnessed to cause great harm in the wrong hands. Cocaine helped alleviate pain in the sickest people among us, but it also destroyed families when it was abused."

"And we stopped using it because of that fact," Trevor

replied. "Are you advocating for the legalization of cocaine?"

"No," I stammered. I wasn't a professional spokesperson, despite the government's attempts to turn me into one. "I'm just saying that people like Sigmund Freud used it to prodigious effect to make some of the greatest breakthroughs in psychology that we've ever known. Heck, Sherlock Holmes used it to solve cases in his novels, but in the wrong hands, it destroyed people."

"So...faekind like cocaine, then?" He leaned closer. I recognized the look in his eyes. He smelled blood and was going in for the kill. I was too tired to avoid walking into the trap.

"Absolutely not. I'm just saying that you're focusing on the destructive nature of magic, but there is great restorative power to it as well. If you look at everything as a threat, then everything becomes a threat. But the fae have the power to be saviors as well."

Trevor tapped his pen on a legal pad on his crossed knee. "And what about you, Rose?"

"What about me?"

"Are you a threat, or a savior?"

I sighed for a moment, trying to catch my breath and think. Despite all my practice, I wasn't good on the spot. I thought back on all of Queen Aine's teachings, to all the lessons where she trained me up to be a queen, and back to Persephone, who had the grace and elegance of a well-worn ruler. They would eat this stupid man for breakfast.

He tapped a notecard on his knee. "We're waiting, Rose."

I took another breath and felt the tenseness in my shoulders loosen. "I'm neither. I'm just a girl—a woman—from Sacramento. I just want to be left alone, as do the fae."

My eyes turned steely. "You are treating me and treating the fae as the enemy, but they saved the whole world, if you remember. They protected you, even though they didn't have to, from a great threat."

"Yes, you say that." He kicked back, stretching out his legs. "But any evidence of this 'great threat' you speak of magically disappeared without a trace, and your army vanished into the sky before they could be questioned. Convenient, don't you think?"

I laughed at the insinuation. "Absolutely not. I find it very inconvenient. I would like them to come forth and defend themselves. I would love to have Nimue's body so that I could prove everything I'm saying—but you can trust me on this: If we wanted to attack humanity, then you would already be gone."

"All right!" Chelle shouted from offstage. Her silhouette stomped towards us. "This interview is over, Trevor!"

He popped up. Trevor was much shorter than he looked onscreen. He was half hair, and a quarter head, with stubby little legs and arms sticking out from them, like a Funko Pop come to life.

"You promised us half an hour!" Trevor whined like a little baby. "It's barely been twenty minutes."

Chelle moved back her hat to reveal a hissing pile of snakes sprouting from her head. Albie, our favorite of the snakes, snapped at the douchey anchor with his single fang. "Are we going to have a problem?"

Trevor shrunk back, his eyes wide. "No, of course not."

"It's pathetic how much you fear us." Chelle took my arm. "Come on, Rose. Let's get that gunk off your face."

"I can finish," I replied. "Let me finish."

She shook her head. "I could see it in your eyes. You were about to say something that would make us look like the violent monsters that we very much aren't."

"I'm sorry," I said, ending her march. "I didn't mean to. It's just...people like him make me so angry."

Chelle's hard jaw softened into a small smile. "Now you know how I feel, but I can't just go taking it out on everybody, now can I? Especially not on national television."

"No, I guess not."

All I wanted was five minutes alone with Chelle where we weren't rushing from one place to another, or so tired that we could barely do more than collapse into each other's arms. We had been living together since Nox brought her back to life for me, but it didn't feel like we had a minute to ourselves since the news of my victory over Nimue went public and *The Sacramento Beat* tracked me down. Since then, I'd been pulled in a hundred different directions with everyone asking for a piece of me.

From the side of the stage a black-suited man in big sunglasses came over. "Ms. Briar, your car is waiting."

I sighed. "How many more interviews do we have today, Agent Edwards?"

The man looked down at his phone. "Three more, all radio. We can record them from the studio back at base, but we need to get moving."

The FBI promised to protect us—Chelle and I—if we cooperated with them, and with dozens of protesters outside my window every day, it was hard to turn them down, so we didn't. I have regretted it ever since, as they, more than anyone else, made me a symbol for faekind, even though I didn't have a drop of fae blood in my whole body.

I pecked Chelle on the cheek. "Go home and get some rest. I'll be back soon, and maybe we can get five minutes to spend with each other."

"I'll order some food and have it ready. Maybe I'll even draw you a bubble bath." She squeezed my hand.

"You're the best." I kissed her full on the lips. It was just as wonderful the thousandth time as it was the first. "I love you."

CHAPTER 2
RED

It had been three months, best I could guess, and I felt no closer to finding the wicked witch Nimue than when I used Persephone's Obsidian Spindle to cross half the galaxy in search of her. Granted, Nox told me that using the portal would do little but get me closer to the Dark Planet so that I could continue my search, but I didn't think I would have to jump between a half dozen systems in the past few months.

Of course, I could be completely wrong with how long it had been since I left Earth. It wasn't like every planet had the same number of days in their months, or the same number of months in their years. Some spun slower and others faster than Earth, and I hadn't brought a watch, so I had to make do with my best guess.

I didn't even know where in the universe I was anymore. I spent my time jumping from one planet's Obsidian Spindle to another, and then finding the gods on that planet to point me in the right direction. Some were helpful, many were not, and none knew where to find the Dark Planet the Faceless Woman called home, though I had the distinct impression they were holding out on me.

My last jump was the most infuriating because I appeared on a planet I had been to before, one of the first planets I visited after I left the Underworld. I recognized the deeply industrialized world that cast out from the edge of the cliff where Rama had built the Obsidian Spindle of his planet.

Though to call it his planet was something of a misnomer. He didn't build it any more than I could build a rock. He merely laid a claim on it, and nobody else challenged him.

Many planets had no god on them, and some had several, but most only had one. Most gods preferred to live in the Celestial Realm with their kind, but just like humans enjoyed owning beach houses and mountain cabins, the gods collected planets across the cosmos. The more powerful the god, the more planets they laid claim to, while the most powerful controlled their own realm, like Nox and Hypnos.

Rama wasn't particularly powerful by the standard of gods, but I had jumped between three of his worlds on my travels already, and I was getting the distinct impression he was leading me in circles. I didn't like playing games, and it was time he knew that about me.

I reached into my coin purse and sorted out a collection of paper money and coins that I acquired during my last trip to Servasi 9 before making my way down the mountain cliff towards the city. The entire world operated on a single grid, with trains so fast they could take you halfway across the planet in a matter of minutes. I didn't need to go that far, or at least I hoped I didn't. With any luck Rama would be in roost at the highest bar in the capital, above the central hub that supplied power for the whole city.

I hopped on a local bus and took it into the city.

"Where are you going?" the elderly bus driver asked me, his syllables foreign and guttural.

One of the advantages of being a construction of the gods, a soul made whole by Hypnos as a gift for helping him save the Dream Realm, was that I understood every language, even ones I had never heard before. "The Haitt district, please."

He nodded. "When your stop comes up, just pull the lever on the edge of the door."

His face flickered as he turned back to face the front. Nobody on Servasi 9 actually had to work, as most jobs had been automated away long ago. But people liked interacting with other humans, so they built holograms into all the electronic workers so people would feel more comfortable and wouldn't question too deeply the dystopian nightmare they lived in.

The city of Chippara looked like an intricate microchip from above, but on the ground it was little more than blurs of whites, yellows, and reds. Living quarters spread across every inch of the city, mixed with little eateries and other services, which were the only places real humans actually worked anymore, and even then, only because they wanted to have a purpose in life aside from wasting away. Those who owned the little restaurants around town were appreciated. While robotic cuisine was fine, there was no variety to it. You could get the exact same hamburger anywhere in the world, which was convenient if you liked that kind of thing, but sometimes you wanted something different. That's where humans found their niche, and could charge a premium for it, too.

The further we moved into the city, the denser and higher the buildings grew. The bus turned down a busy intersection full of self-driving cars and I saw my destination, an enormous building, summited with a neon blue roof that pointed into the black sky, spidering out electricity to hundreds of substations, which relayed commands to ancillary hubs around the city, which in turn relayed power to thousands of buildings in their districts.

Every city had a power hub, but the one in Chippara was the largest on the planet, and atop it the richest and most powerful beings dined and made merry, including Rama. Of all the planets he claimed for himself, this was the most decadent, and the one that he was the proudest to control.

I pulled the lever half a mile from the building and the bus screeched to a stop by the time I reached the sliding doors and hopped out. The bus sped up moments after I exited, its doors slamming closed and nearly took my red cape along with it.

I wasn't often impressed, but the magnitude of the glowing building, with little circuits firing along the exterior of it all the way up, was enough to make even me marvel. It was surrounded by impressive structures, and still it stood out from them all.

A cadre of holographic guards milled around the shimmering white lobby when I entered. It was almost impossible to know them to be fakes unless you stared closely enough to notice their nearly imperceptible refresh rate of their bodies.

"How can I help you?" a dark-skinned woman made of hard angles asked.

"I need to see Rama. Is he upstairs?"

"Lord Rama is entertaining tonight. He is indisposed as of now. If you'd like to make an appointment, he has an opening in sixteen years from tonight."

I smirked. "Oh, I'm sorry. I didn't mean that I wanted to

see him. I have a dinner reservation, and I wanted to know if I would have the honor of basking in his presence."

Servasi 9 wasn't a planet where people had reason to lie often, so you could short-circuit a hologram by simply telling a big enough fib. They were smart, but they weren't programmed to react with mistrust.

The angled woman's neck twitched to the side, and she smiled. "Well, in that case I'm very happy to tell you that he is upstairs, in the rooftop lounge."

The gods were various levels of discrete, depending on the situation, and there was barely a reason to hide in this place. People didn't worship gods here. They worshipped technology. It was one thing Rama loved most about the place, and why none of the other gods came within two systems of it.

The counter in front of the guard opened, and two small slots appeared in the emptiness. "Please insert payment for your meal."

Very few people could afford to dine in such a luxurious place as the rooftop bar. Most people were given just enough to survive, and a single meal in the rooftop lounge cost as much as a month's stipend. Money was how you proved you belonged.

I pulled the coins out of my purse. "I think that should do it."

I didn't have much left after that, but I didn't intend to spend much time on this stupid planet, and if I did, then something would have gone horribly wrong.

The elevator dinged and the doors opened. "Go inside, and you'll be taken right up. Enjoy your dinner."

CHAPTER 3
CHELLE

I didn't like leaving Rose for any reason. Not only did I distrust the FBI with every fiber of my being, but the protests around her appearances were getting worse. There had been over a hundred monsters and fae outside the CBS building this morning when we arrived. By the time I exited the front door, there were over five hundred. The more Rose spoke, the more ire grew between the magical community who both hated being lumped in with the fae and having a human woman speak for them.

Not to mention the counter-protests by humans disgusted by the idea that monsters and magical beings lived among them. They shouted hate-filled slogans and yelled obscenities, hoping to provoke my kind to violence. One day it will work, and I just hoped it wasn't the powder keg that started a war.

There was already legislation running through Congress with competing ideas about how to deal with us, ranging from rounding magical folk up into internment camps to shipping us to Guam and treating it like a penal colony, to providing aid and assistance to integrate us with the rest of society.

That last one was the funniest one to me, because we were already integrated. We were their plumbers, electricians, jewelers, and cooks. Magic fueled some of Earth's technology, and fae folk ran their most profitable companies. They could no easier extradite us to some island as they could ship all the Black people back to Africa.

At least some good came out of it, though. Those of us who felt comfortable enough no longer had to hide in the shadows, and I chose not to wear a wig anymore. Plenty of people turned their heads as I walked down the street, but it was no longer a shocking occasion to see a gorgon on the street, especially in New York City, which had always been a haven for the weird and strange.

The FBI relocated us here after the battle in Switzerland, when Rose agreed to be their mouthpiece in exchange for our protection, a devil's bargain if I ever heard one. Still, I liked New York City more than I thought I would, and it was nice to be within walking distance of a half dozen comic book stores. There weren't many in Sacramento.

I wasn't in the mood for comics as I walked past Midtown Comics and turned up from Times Square towards 47th Street. I hated the middle of the city, but that's where most of the media outlets were located, and so we were there a lot, enough that I knew the area by heart.

I spent too many bored hours walking the streets and gazing into the windows of the stores, but today I was there to buy a diamond ring I had custom made for Rose. I was sick of people calling her Miss, and I was determined to make an honest woman of her, as they say.

Zarfo Isbett owned one of the most prestigious stores in

the Diamond District, and I thought of her often when people screamed about magical beings being leeches on society. She was a harpy disguised in a full burka and had lived in the Diamond District for a hundred years, taking on the persona of her own mother and grandmother before they "died."

"Good morning, Ingrid," I said to her, too wary of a browsing couple looking at rings to use her real name. "How's business?"

She jutted her chin at the couple. "They're cool, Chelle. A pair of gnolls looking for an engagement ring. Most of my business comes from monsters these days." She beckoned me into the back of the store, where she reached down into a cabinet and pulled out a red felt jewelry case. "I hope you're happy with my work."

Inside the case was a two-carat diamond surrounded by five smaller diamonds. The band was rose gold in the shape of a thorny rose entwined with a snake. "It's beautiful."

She picked it up so I could see the inscription inside: *I will love you to the end of the universe, no matter where our souls roam.*

"It was quite a bit to inscribe, you know," Zarfo grumbled. "Usually people put 'I love you' or something simple like that."

"Yeah, well our love has never been simple." I looked up from the ring, smiling. "This is perfect, thank you."

I pulled out a credit card that I'd gotten specifically for this occasion and prayed it would swipe through without issue. The FBI had us both on their payroll, but even with their money I didn't have nearly enough to cover the cost of the ring. This was easily the biggest purchase of my life, but Rose was worth going into debt for. Wasn't it funny, though, that the first thing we do when starting our life with somebody is go into debt buying a nice ring?

The till rang and the receipt printed out. For a moment, my eyes went wide as I wondered what I had done, but that quickly faded as she handed me the box and the receipt. "I hope she says yes."

I smiled at her. "She will."

She had trekked into Hell to save me, and I dove into the Dream Realm to save her. There was nothing we wouldn't do for each other. Our souls were already bound together. Now, it was just making it official.

I had always thought marriage was stupid, especially seeing how poorly matched my mother and father were until he finally cut tail and ran. They made each other miserable, and I never wanted that for myself. However, looking at Rose, even thinking about her, I couldn't imagine not wanting to be with her for the rest of my life, and beyond.

I walked back onto the sidewalk with a big smile on my face and glanced at my watch. I had barely used up any time. Rose would still be hours at the station. Maybe I would head to Midtown Comics after all and pick up my pulls for the week. Yes, comics and proposing to the love of my life. It was going to be a very good day.

CHAPTER 4
ARIEL

No matter how long I spent at the bottom of the sea, I never got tired of exploring the ocean floor to find new trinkets. Sailors dropped interesting things from their boats, and I scooped up those that the mermaids didn't claim.

Not that there were many sailors these days. They feared crossing the Forgotten Sea and didn't understand that if they didn't give the mermaids a reason to attack, they wouldn't...most of the time. I couldn't deny that there were a few times when our people got overzealous, but those incidents were few and far between.

I had lived under the sea for 300 years, and the mermaids had never been anything but pleasant to me even though I was an outsider. They never complained when I scavenged the boats on the bottom of the ocean, or laid claim to some thingamajig that might have rightfully been theirs.

It might have been that my adopted mother was the queen of the mermaids, of course, but I like to believe that I would have been allowed to live in peace even if she hadn't taken me in.

"*Lux,*" I said as I swam through two rocky outcroppings where algae had grown thick. I was on the search for a boat that sank around the time I'd been brought to the sea, drowned in a battle between the queen's forces and a group of usurpers desperate to keep her off the throne.

Darkness collapsed around me, so thick it nearly extinguished my small light. There were few places more oppressively black than Nox's cave, but this was close.

"*Splendens procedit,*" I whispered, and my light flickered, fighting against the abyss until it latched onto a piece of rotten wood in the distance. The mast of a boat appeared as I approached. Etched in the back of the boat was carved a single word: *Aveline.*

This is it. A shipwreck long thought lost, but I knew that nothing was lost in the Forgotten Sea, only faded from memory.

I kicked my feet towards the hull, where a huge hole led into the wonders inside. Not having fins was the worst part of living under the sea. I fashioned some flippers, but it wasn't the same. My brothers and sisters could propel themselves quickly with little effort. They were graceful and beautiful, twisting and turning like they were born for the water, which, of course, they were. I was born on land, but that's not where I belonged. Here, under the sea, I could be free.

"There you are!" A shrill voice cut through the water. I turned to see my mother's most trusted advisor, Cefus, darting towards me. "Didn't your mother tell you never to go past the Golden Cove?"

I shrugged. "She's told me not to go a lot of places, and that didn't stop me. What do you want, Cefus?"

"Your mother has been looking for you all day. She has received a very distressing message from Queen Aine. You are to return to the castle at once." His mouth opened wide, and a shriek went through the air. Within moments a chariot shot towards us, pulled by two dolphins. "There isn't a moment to lose, Miss. She really was quite insistent."

I looked back at the ship. Next time I slipped through the castle guards, I would come back again.

"Yes, Cefus," I said, swimming towards the chariot. "Whatever my mother needs."

I turned off the light in my hand and when I joined him on the seat, he shut the door. The dolphins didn't need any instructions. Cefus always found me easily when I ventured too far from the castle. He could canvas a much larger area in a shorter time than I could with my stubby little legs.

Still, I did okay scavenging the bottom of the ocean. I found thingamajigs and whatsamathings aplenty, along with all sorts of spoons, forks, chests, and other objects which I knew from my years on the surface. I'd forgotten almost everything from those days, and the little trinkets I found connected me back to it and helped me remember, even if I'd never totally fit in there after my time under the sea.

It took less than half the time to return to the castle as it had for me to find the ship in the first place and watching the ocean speed past reminded me just how ill-equipped I was for living under the ocean. It wouldn't have been possible at all, though, if we didn't live in the Dream Realm, where souls could live just about anywhere until they were dusted and vanished into the ether.

When we arrived at the palace entrance, Cefus showed me out of the chariot and through the coral doors of my mother's castle. It would never be mine, I knew that. She would never give her kingdom to an adopted daughter, even if I was the most loyal of all her children.

"Your Majesty," Cefus bellowed upon our entrance into the throne room. He was always so smug when he brought me back, and he kept his swagger for days afterwards. "Your wayward daughter has returned."

"Where did you find her?" my mother asked in an exasperated tone.

"In the abyss, out past the Golden Pond."

She growled. "Yes, you would go there, wouldn't you? I thought we agreed that you needed to temper your wanderlust."

"I'm sorry, Mother. I will do better."

"You will have your chance to prove that, but not just yet. Queen Aine has requested your presence in the Emerald City."

"The Emerald City?" My body began to shake in fear. Though souls didn't have hearts, I swore I still felt one beating in my body. "The surface? I can't. You—please don't make me do this. I have been safe under the sea for these long years. Please don't send me back to the surface."

Mother's eyes narrowed. "I'm afraid this can't wait. The goddess Nox has disappeared, and the queen believes you can help with a matter of great importance in her absence."

"Why me?"

"Because, my love." A ghastly smile rose on her gray face. "You are the only surviving ruler of the Land of Oz, and as such, you have knowledge that nobody else in the whole of Urgu has. We must maintain good relations with our friends on the surface, don't you think?"

"Yes, but I—"

"Good, good." She flapped her fishy fingers at me. "Then I don't want to hear another word about it. Don't you want to be a good girl?"

I bit my lip. I was scared out of my mind to return to the

surface, but I couldn't help my deep-seated desire to do what mother said. "Yes, I will go."

"Lovely," she said. "Now, come here and let me say my goodbyes."

I expected her to place her hands around my shoulders, but instead she placed them on my head, and the heat that shot from them after a moment felt familiar.

"Good, girl. Now, forget all you saw today, except for my commands, and prepare for your journey."

The heat abated, and I smiled at her. "Yes, Mother."

CHAPTER 5
NIMUE

I had been living in the muck for months, and the Faceless Woman did little more than stare at me in silence. At least I thought she was staring. She didn't have a face. All I could tell for sure was that her blank face followed whenever I moved. If she was the most powerful witch in the universe, one that even the gods feared, then I hoped she could track me with her mind. Otherwise, she couldn't be that powerful.

"Yes, I can track you with my mind." The raspy voice rested on the air, but it didn't come from the Faceless Woman. "I can hear every thought rattling around inside your brain. Disappointing. The first guest in ages, and you could not be more boring."

She hadn't acknowledged me or responded to me in months, and now she wanted to insult me?

"Well, I wouldn't be boring," I snarled, "if you would teach me something."

"How can I teach an ant to be an eagle? It would be a waste of both our time."

"Are you calling me weak?"

"Well, yes, dear. Of course I am."

"I am not weak! I was Queen of Oz. I had the blessing of Hera and Epiales. I held the darkness in my hands and commanded it."

"Yes, yes. I'm quite aware that you needed the gods to obtain your power, which is exactly what makes you weak, and exactly why you believe you aren't. The ant can lift many times its body weight, but it can easily be crushed underfoot, just as you would fall to even the weakest god."

A fire grew in my belly that I hadn't felt in a while. I promised to be humble and subservient to the Faceless Woman lest she turn me into dust, but I didn't care how much she would punish me...nobody called me weak.

"I call you weak," her voice cracked. She'd moved behind me before my eyes could even register it. When I turned, she reached her hand into my chest and ripped out my beating heart. "And now I have proved just how pathetic you really are."

"How?" I choked as I stumbled backward, blood pouring from my chest. "I thought—"

"It was nothing to me."

"I have never see—seen—"

"Another human with so much power? That is because my power doesn't come from a blessing, but the source of all things. True power comes not from the gods, but from the primordial forces that flow through the world. The gods are merely a conduit, and a bad one at that. Anyone who can tap into the forces themselves will be more powerful than them and their chosen. That is your first lesson. Whether you get a second is up to you."

"Please..." My body convulsed.

She looked down at her hand, covered in my blood, and reached into herself, pulling out her own black heart. Black ichor streamed down her body. "Do you need one of these? Interesting. I thought they were just decoration."

"Don't...mock...please."

She knelt to me. "Do you see the power you could have if you stopped thinking so small? Reach out, in your final moments, and feel the forces of the universe flowing through you. If you have even a spark of the divine inside of you, then I will save your life, or, more accurately, you will save yourself."

My body quaked with the throes of death. I had made a terrible mistake coming here, and now I would die in this horrible place, when I could have been quite happy back in the Fairy Realm, or on Urgu, or even Earth.

I had no choice but to do as the Faceless Woman said and turn to the primordial forces for help. I knew how it felt to wield the power of the gods, and the power of the darkness, but I had no idea what it would feel like to wield the power of the forces themselves.

My body shook in its final death throes, and I felt my soul leaving my body. In that moment a charge jolted through me, as if the universe reached through and hugged me, pulling me into its eternal bosom. It was gone a second later, and my soul leapt back in my body. The Faceless Woman no longer had my heart in her hands. The wound on my chest had closed up, not even leaving a scar.

I gasped for breath. "Thank you."

"That wasn't me," she said, sticking her own black heart back in her chest. "That was you, in a moment of clarity, feeling the divine force flow through you. That is why I am so frightening to the gods, because humanity should not be able to access that type of power."

"I very much want it," I said. "Please, teach me."

"Not yet," she replied. "I require payment first."

"I have nothing. Save for the clothes on my back."

"That is not the type of payment I need. You will help me reconstruct my face, return what the gods have stolen from me, and for each piece you bring back, I will teach you more about the primordial forces that grant us unlimited power."

"Anything," I breathed, leaning my head back. "I would do anything to feel that power again."

CHAPTER 6

CHELLE

It was getting dark by the time I left Midtown with a fistful of new comics. I never much appreciated comics before I moved to New York, but with a thousand superhero movies coming out nearly every month, it seemed, and even more on television and streaming apps, I decided to give them a shot. I was thoroughly happy that I did, especially since my tastes splintered out from the standard Marvel and DC flair into more independent books.

Reading was more of Rose's thing, but now that I spent most of my days waiting for her one way or another, I needed something to fill the hours. Novels were fine, but I was in the 25 percent of people who literally had no imagination, so they were only ever little more than words on a page. Comics showed you exactly what you were supposed to see.

I knew from movies and television that the New York Subway system was a freakshow, but after magical folk were outed, the oddities of the subway became even more pronounced. Drag queens still mingled with homeless drifters, who rubbed elbows with orthodox Muslims, but now elves, dwarves, demons, dragonborn, and all manner of magical beings mixed among them.

To the city's credit, they were incredibly tolerant of their new inhabitants, much more so than most of the country, save for bigger cities that already had a diverse mix of people inside of them. There were safe havens all over the world in smaller cities and pockets that accepted us, but they were few and far between.

I took the subway downtown and got off at 14th street, where I picked up falafel and a lamb gyro platter from our favorite restaurant. Rose deserved more of an occasion for my proposal, but I couldn't plan for us going out without a small army of FBI officers locking the place down and blowing the surprise. Rose was barely able to leave our apartment with all the people trying to get a piece of her these days, so we took our meals at home. Since neither of us cooked, that meant a lot of takeout.

It was funny to think that Rose needed protection. Rose, who was blessed by Hypnos and Persephone both; who ruled the Land of Oz and proxied for the Queen of the Underworld; who saved three realms, and who journeyed into Hell to save me. Rose could snap her fingers and disintegrate an attacker in an instant, though that wasn't something we broadcast to people. If it got out that my girlfriend was vaporizing people, it would be bad for the cause of magical tolerance.

I couldn't deny that part of me loved the fact that Rose outed us all. It meant I no longer had to live in the shadows, and I could move freely around the world in a way I never thought would be possible. Even with all the risks and the evil looks that people gave me, it was worth it to be able to let my snake hair free and live my truth.

Our apartment building was old, like most everything

in New York City that hadn't been demolished and rebuilt as some sleek, modern monstrosity. The sinks didn't work right, and we were constantly complaining to the landlord about something or another, but I loved the East Village. The apartment was cute, too, even if it was up three flights of stairs.

"Cheyenne! I'm home!" I shouted as I opened the door. A little runt of a dachshund skittered across the hardwood towards me, arooing happily as she leapt on me. I hadn't loved the stupid mutt at first. She was needy and possessive and hated everyone except for me and Rose, but Rose loved her, and so I loved her too, first by the transitive property, and then in my own way.

"Did you miss me?" I squealed in a voice two octaves too high. She leapt up and licked my face as if I had been gone for ten years instead of ten hours. "Yes, I love you, too. Yes, I do."

After a minute she calmed down and went to investigate the food, which I raised into the air to keep from her. I brought it to the kitchen, which was also the living room, and served about six other functions. In Sacramento, we could have gotten a literal penthouse for the price of our tiny apartment.

As I set up for dinner, Cheyenne barked at the door. She was always barking at something. "It's fine, girl. It's probably the neigh—"

After a flash of light, a massive creature, clad all in black from its helmet to its jackboots stood in the doorway.

"Chelle Anderson?" the low voice grumbled.

"Who are you?" I lunged into a fighting stance. "Get out of my house."

The creature ignored my threat and moved closer. "You

are under arrest by the United Federation of Gods for crimes against the Pantheon."

"I never heard of you before but if you want a fight, you got one." My hands filled with fire. *"Turbine Ignis!"* I screamed and shot a torrent of fire. When I finally dropped my arms, the creature stepped out of the steam without a scratch.

"Your resistance will be noted." It clapped its hands together, and bright blue shackles collapsed around my hands and feet, dropping me to the ground.

"Get these off me!"

Cheyenne nipped at the thing's heels as it stepped through the room, unphased by her tiny attacks. I clawed and kicked, but it picked me up anyway. It slammed a glowing red disc on its chest, and we vanished, the sound of Cheyenne's barking fell away into silence.

CHAPTER 7
RED

The elevator doors slid open into pure opulence. Gold, copper, and silver furniture filled the room, emulating the circuit board design of the rest of the city. All throughout the room, tables rose like nodes on a motherboard. Most of the denizens of Rama's world wore drab black suits and dresses, but the rooftop bar was an explosion of color, frilly collars, and over-the-top designs. They were every bit the royalty garb I remembered from my time in the Emerald City, where members of court tried to outdo the garish dress of the others to prove their immense wealth.

I stepped through the flock of peacocks nesting around the room and found a seat at the bar. A rosy-cheeked woman with an overly-powdered face and white wig turned to me.

"What can I get you, stranger?"

"Rama," I replied.

She smiled, revealing two rows of gold teeth. "That's not a drink, hon. That's a person."

I leaned my elbows on the table. "Actually, he's a god. Where is he?"

"Seems like if you're meant to see him, you would know that, wouldn't you? Do I need to call security?"

I shook my head, pulling back my cape to reveal the dagger sheathed on my belt. "Not unless you want to cause a scene. It would be easier if you just answered my question, and then you and your friends can go on playing dress-up." She chuckled. "What's so funny?"

Her eyebrow raised. "You think these are my friends? Please. I'm paid to be here and paid well. I don't want any trouble, and I don't want my boss to fire me."

"Your name won't even come up," I replied.

"And you won't cause a scene?"

"I can't promise that, but I will definitely cause a scene if you don't tell me. Then all these hideously dressed rich people will have to find another place to drink."

She rolled her eyes. "Behind the bar, third door on the left. Password is 'virtue.'"

I winked. "That wasn't so hard, was it?"

Three illuminated lines lit the way to the hallway, and as I walked down it the crowd thinned. I was alone when I reached the room at the end of it. I knocked on the door and a red eye popped and scanned me.

"Password."

"Virtue," I replied. It was a little on the nose, given that what Rama was known for was virtue and honesty. Of course, that was his outward appearance. I knew all too well that even the most virtuous gods were sinful and vain.

After a moment the door clicked and slid open. Rama, blue-skinned and dressed in a three-piece purple suit, inlaid with a pattern of white thorns and flowers, looked up from the scantily-clad women on either side of him and smiled.

"Gabrielle," he said, smirking. "So nice to see you."

The door slid closed. "We need to talk, Rama. You've been sending me in circles since I got here. Why?"

"Well, I thought this was going to be pleasant, but you are being quite rude." He snapped his fingers and the girls slid out of the booth and through the door. "I won't be long, girls. I promise."

I rubbed my finger on the spot between my eyebrows. This wasn't my first encounter with Rama, and each one was equally frustrating. "Talking with you always gives me a migraine. Can you, for once, just give me a straight answer?"

He smiled. "That is the problem with you, my dear. You believe there is one right path, and that somehow you can find it, and walk it, but the universe is a million shades of gray."

"You don't know me at all if you believe I am that naïve."

He placed his arms on either side of the booth, stretching out comfortably. "No? You believed that it would be easy to find the secret doorway into the Dark Planet—a place the gods have kept hidden for thousands of years? You thought you could charm me and get exactly what you wanted without working for it."

"I am not opposed to hard work," I replied. "But I do not like being jerked around. Nox told me th—"

He laughed loudly. "Do you really think that Nox has any weight outside the Dream Realm? The world has moved on since she retreated there. It's been centuries since her name held sway in the universe." He leaned in. "Did you even know your precious Nox was arrested?"

"On what charge?" I asked.

"On the charge of creating you, an abomination. A mortal soul bound by magic, allowed to roam free."

"I was not created by Nox."

"Is that true?" He stroked his chin. "Well, that is interesting, because she is certainly charged with your creation —and that of your friend Chelle, the gorgon half-breed. You don't even know how much of an affront to nature you and she are, do you?"

"Hold your tongue about my friends," I replied, pressing my hand into the daggers in my belt. "I have killed for less."

He laughed again. "I don't fear you, Red Rider. You may scare Persephone, or Hypnos, but I will never trouble myself by fearing your kind. That being said, I will make you a deal."

"Why would I ever make a deal with you?"

"Because I didn't turn you in on sight, and because you are still alive, even though you insult me every time we meet. You might not think much of me, but I value honor and virtue, so I will make you a deal."

"I seem to have no choice, so speak."

"How magnanimous of you." He leaned back and tented his fingers. "Many eons ago, I got in...let's call it a lover's spat...with Kadlu. In retaliation for spurning her, she stole my beloved brahmastra, and I want it back."

"You want me to find a bow for you?"

"Not just any bow, the only weapon befitting a god of my stature. Find this weapon for me, and I will bring you personally to the gate to the Dark Planet."

"Why me?" I asked.

"I have watched you traverse a dozen worlds, skirt death a hundred times, and still survive. If any could be my champion, then it is you."

I thought for a moment. "I don't like being a pawn for the gods, but if that is the only way to find the Dark Planet, then I will do it."

CHAPTER 8
NIMUE

"So..." I started, pressing my hand in my chest to feel my heartbeat. "Does that mean you weren't always like this?"

"Crass," the Faceless Woman replied. "But no. I was not always like this. Once, I was a beautiful woman—born on the same Earth as you came from, in fact—though some thousand years ago. My mother and father, the king and queen, made a deal with a witch, and the price was their first-born child. I was locked away in a castle tower for twenty years and the witch experimented on me, using my body in ways I wouldn't wish on anyone." She stopped for a moment, reflective in a way I had never known her to be. "Eventually I was saved by a prince, and that's where the fairy tale ends for me, I'm afraid."

"Why do you sound so sad about it? Was he crueler than the witch?" I asked.

"Not cruel, just banal. I hate to admit this, but I know you will not judge my lust for power, given that it resides in you, too. When I returned to my kingdom, my parents were so happy, and yet I was hollow inside. The witch was evil, mean, and conniving, but she had a power that my parents couldn't match, and I knew that the only way to protect myself was to gain that power for myself." Her words turned wistful. "I took the witch into my castle as my prisoner. My parents, even my betrothed, demanded her head, but I kept her safe in exchange for her teaching me all she knew about witchcraft."

"And she did," I added.

"Of course she did. I thought I would be happy then, but when I heard of greater power in a nearby kingdom, I demanded my husband find that sorceress for me. I brought her into my confidence, and she showed me more, but there were limits to even her power. She told me of knowledge kept only by the gods and so I found myself walking through the forest, trying to summon Hestia, Oko, Geb, Artio, or Sucellus. Finally Pan heard my prayers, and came to me. He taught me how to love truly and blessed me as his own. My power grew, but I felt the limit of it in the limits of Pan himself. I learned from him that the power of the gods came from the forces themselves, the primordial energy that made up the universe, and I demanded to know how to access it."

"But he didn't tell you."

She shook her head. "The thought of a mortal wielding the true power of the gods unmoored him. He left me, taking his blessing with him. Undeterred, I traveled the world, abandoning my duties to my kingdom to find a way to access the forces. It was then that I discovered my first Spindle and used it to travel between worlds, capturing knowledge from different planets, until I arrived at the Celestial Realm."

"What's that?"

"Where the gods live, and where they all originated. I snuck through their world. I was only an ant to them, so they paid me no mind, until I found a way to harness the forces for my own."

"That's incredible."

"The gods did not think so. They suddenly took notice of me and were not happy that a mortal could learn their secrets."

"Why?"

"The only thing that keeps us under their thumb is that we are weak, brittle, and die quickly. There are more of us than there are of them. If humanity harnessed the power of the gods, they would no longer be able to subjugate us. That made me dangerous, so they made an example of me."

"Horrible," I said, with as much sympathy as I could muster.

"They could not kill me, nor did they want to. I would be a symbol of their power, and what happened when one tried to touch the power of a god. Instead, they took my eyes, my ears, my nose, and my mouth. They locked them away in the four corners of the universe, but even locked in this place, I have learned their whereabouts."

"Then why don't you simply track them down?"

Her head sank. "I cannot leave this planet, and even if I could, they watch my movements like a hawk. I could not step foot through the secret doorway even if I tried, and in my weakened state I would be nothing against them. However...you are still mortal. They take no notice of you. You can find my treasures and return them to me. When I am assembled again, I will unlock the same power in you, and we can take on the gods and give their power to the masses."

I didn't have to think about it. I hated the gods. I hated everything about them, and the ability to wreak havoc on their lives brought a smile to my face. "I want nothing more than to knock those gods down a few pegs."

"Indeed." She touched my forehead. I jumped, considering that the last time she reached for me, she'd torn the heart from my chest. This time she used just the tip of her finger, and a cool breeze rushed through me. "There. I have given you my blessing. It is not as powerful as receiving your magic from the forces, but it is a far cry better than where you stand now. Over time I will teach you how to do all the things the gods kept hidden from you."

I stood up, feeling the power rush through me. For so long I had only had the power of the darkness, a piteous force that demanded fealty in order to work. But this power, I was in complete control of it.

"Lightning strike!" I shouted, and a surge of pure energy shot through my body as a crackle of lightning electrified a tree up ahead, sending it up in flames. "Rainstorm!" Clouds formed above and rain doused the tree, putting out the fire and replacing it with a gentle steam that flowed from a puddle.

"How does it feel?" the Faceless Woman asked.

"Amazing," I replied. "I forgot how good it felt to wield the power of the gods."

She stood to match my height and took my hands in hers. "Even with this power, you must be careful. The worst atrocities in the whole universe, those that the gods fear more than anything, are trapped here on this planet, cut off from the rest of the universe. You must be careful, or you will surely fail on your journey before you even regain one of my senses. Trust no one."

"Where will I go first?" I asked.

"The capital," she replied. "The first piece you must track down is held by the king of this planet, Hastur. A pompous man, appointed by the gods, who wears my nose around his neck as a symbol of his power."

"A king," I repeated. "How will I get to him?"

"Go to the nearest town," she said, "and find a woman named Cassandra. Tell her that I have sent you. She will arrange passage for you, and an invite to one of the king's many galas, where you will take back my nose. Do you understand?"

I nodded. "Yes, my master. Your will be done."

She placed a hand on my head. "Now go."

CHAPTER 9

ARIEL

The last time I was on the surface, my mother had been kidnapped and I was thrown into the sea, never to be seen again. It was Nox that found me floating in the briny deep and brought me to Ursula, who took pity on me, and allowed me to live with her.

For the past three centuries, I had been protected by the mermaids. No one would dare try to dust me with the entirety of Ursula's army ready to defend me. Now, my adopted mother asked me to abandon that safety to make a visit to the Emerald City.

And I would go because I was a dutiful daughter. I would not complain. I would simply go and make my presence known. The Queen of Oz would have a chance to say her piece, and then I would return to the deep forever, having fulfilled my duty.

"Are you ready, princess?" Cefus asked from the doorway of my bedchamber. I had spent many days locked inside, desperate to defy my mother's wishes and search the deep, dark ocean. One day, I would see beyond the castle's boundaries and explore the darkness that lived through the nooks and crannies at the bottom of the sea.

"Just a minute," I replied.

I reached into the bottom drawer and pulled out a sequined white dress. It was the dress I was wearing when I fell into the sea, and the only thing that even resembled the type of gown I would find on the surface. I didn't remember much about the surface, but I knew that a princess didn't wear rags to the Emerald Palace.

The dress still fit, as time didn't move forward in the Dream Realm. When I was done, I looked at myself in my vanity mirror before opening the door again. The dress was constricting and made it hard to swim or move at all. That was the point, though. Royalty didn't move. The world moved around them.

I balled up the bottom of my dress in my fists and struggled to keep up with Cefus, who showed no mercy for my puny legs as he zipped through the palace. When we exited the castle, he held open the door to the front door for me.

"When you get to the surface, use the spell '*siccum*' and it will dry you completely. Then, touch your hair and say '*recta*' to straighten your hair. Finally, touch your face and say '*colore*' and it will make you up for a royal procession."

I hadn't worried about presentation in eons, but it was all the Emerald City cared about, at least in my fuzzy memory. One of the most freeing parts of living under the sea was that the mermaids simply didn't care about how I looked.

"Thank you," I replied.

Cefus closed the door to the carriage and the dolphins started us towards the surface. As we moved, my stomach sank further and further into my feet. That's when I realized that I had no shoes.

If I jumped out of the carriage right now, I could swim back home...but then I would have to deal with my mother's disappointment for the rest of my days.

No, I had to keep going, shoeless and alone.

As the dark blue ocean bled into lighter tones, the mermaids hidden by the dark made themselves known, and a swarm of them parted so we could travel through towards the surface. My ears popped twice before the shimmer of light from the sun peeked through the water, and then, all at once, we broke through the surface with a splash.

It was so bright above the water that even with my eyes closed it was overwhelming. It took several minutes before I could focus on the shore. A green city rose high into the sky, shimmering and beautiful just like I remembered from my youth. Weird, silly looking birds floated through the air, and long carriages not pulled by any animals passed along the ground. And sure enough, the Obsidian Spindle stood immoveable across the Rainbow Bridge that arched over the Forgotten Sea.

When the dolphins finally reached the shore, the door popped open to let me out. I stepped onto the sand, and there was a heat I hadn't felt in many years. The bottom of the ocean was a frigid place, and the surface had a warmth that I had forgotten I missed against my skin.

My feet shook with trepidation, and, against my every instinct, I willed them to keep moving forward. *"Siccum,"* I mumbled, waving my hands over my dress. As I did, the water leached from my body and my dress, leaving it dry, but ruffled. My dress had a thousand wrinkles in it, and my hair was frizzy and unkempt.

"Recta." I ran my hands down my hair and body, and the wrinkles vanished. When I patted my head again, the stray

hairs were gone, and all that remained was the perfectly straight hair that I remembered having once.

"*Colore.*" I placed my hands on my face, and felt something powder passing across my skin, then something drew on my cheeks and eyelids.

"Are you Princess Ariel?" The man who spoke to me was plump, and wore a green tunic emblazoned with a fairy on the front. "We have been expecting you."

I nodded. "I am she."

He gave me a curt smile. "If you follow me, I'll lead you to your limo."

"Limo?"

"A lot has changed since the last time you were on the surface. I'll fill you in on the way to the palace." He glanced at my bare feet. "We'll get you some proper footwear as well, and a new dress, too." Reaching into his tunic, he pulled out a silver tiara, adorned with diamonds across its face. "I believe this is yours, Your Majesty. A gift from the queen, on the occasion of your return to the surface."

I took the tiara and my eyes filled with tears. "This was given to me by my mother."

Maybe it would not be so bad after all, being on the surface, especially if everyone was filled with so much kindness.

CHAPTER 10

ROSE

I hated being on radio almost as much as I hated being on camera, but at least with radio you didn't have to worry what you were doing with your hands or if your makeup was running, and there weren't a thousand hot lights blaring down on you, making you feel like you're in the Sandlands back in Urgu.

"I need a weekend off, Derek," I said to the FBI agent in the passenger's seat after my interviews were over. "I've done fifty hits in the past two weeks, and I'm completely drained."

I used to think that disc jockeys only working 2-4 hours a day meant they were lazy but after being on interview after interview, talking nonstop for days on end, I had a new respect for their craft, and how hard it was to figure out how to talk for hours on end.

At least I didn't have to do much drive-time radio. Shows like "Spongy and the Tits" or "Balls and the Ferret" didn't have much use for intelligent conversation. If they wanted to talk to me, it was to discuss how hot I was, or ask if they could squeeze my breasts, or try to convince me to jelly-wrestle a prostitute, or something equally asinine and degrading. The FBI treated me like a piece of meat, but at least they protected me from those kinds of interviews for the most part.

"We have a lot of interviews scheduled for the next couple of weeks, but I promise we'll give you a whole week off once this cools down."

I laughed. "Do you really think this is ever going to cool down? Or are you lying to me?"

"I think I'm mostly lying to myself, ma'am," Derek said. I stared daggers at him. "I'll see what I can do to get you next weekend off, okay?"

"That's all I ask."

I really needed time with Chelle and to gather my thoughts. There was something she needed to tell me; something needling her, but every time she tried to have a conversation with me, I either fell asleep on her or had to leave for some stupid event or another. When I wasn't doing interviews, I was the guest of honor at some gala, or had a meeting with one dignitary or another.

I didn't want any of this. How had it become my life?

I suppose it didn't much matter how it happened, just that it happened, and now I had to make the best of it and make sure I didn't neglect Chelle in the process. I was determined to get home before the food got cold tonight and have more than ten minutes with her before we fell asleep. Chelle wasn't a patient woman, but had been so great with all of this, and from now on I was determined to take back my life with her. She was everything to me, and I treated her like trash. I'd traveled to Hell to save her, and I couldn't even find an evening to spend with her? She literally came back from the dead for me.

I stopped a block from my apartment and picked up a

bunch of roses for her, plus a box of chocolates. It was a corny gesture, but it was a gesture nonetheless. It would be the start of a new life for the two of us.

The protests outside my apartment building had died down so I could enter without having my entourage push through a hundred people and magical beings telling me how awful I was for simply existing.

Being popular and powerful meant you had to eat a lot of crow, apparently. It took a lot of restraint to not simply snap my fingers and burn them all to cinder. Persephone's power still flowed through me, and beneath it, Hypnos's struggled to get out as well. It would be so easy to destroy every one of my nay-sayers and yet I kept my cool. I didn't even get a medal for it.

"Chelle! I'm home!" I called from the entryway. Cheyenne rushed towards me, but she wasn't happy like she always was. He hackles were up, and she was barking nonstop. "What's wrong, girl?"

I reached my hand out and let her smell it, and when she realized it was me her barks turned to whimpers as she licked my fingers. I placed the chocolate and roses on the coffee table and looked around. Something was wrong. I picked up Cheyenne and searched the apartment for Chelle. I expected to find her in the tub, passed out in bed, or something, but she was just...gone.

When I tried to call her, her phone rang from next to a red box on the table. I swiped it open, but all I found was her text message to me: *I love you.* I set Cheyenne down and picked up the red box. Flipping it open, I began to cry in both sadness and joy. It was an engagement ring, no doubt about it, and that made me even more scared. There was no way she would leave, knowing I would be home soon, unless something was incredibly wrong. Not if she was going to propose.

I pulled the ring out of the box and slid it over my finger. It fit perfectly. It might not have been right, but I wasn't going to live without her as my fiancée for another moment. *Yes, Chelle. I will marry you, but I have to find you first.*

CHAPTER II
ARIEL

I forgot how much I hated heels and couldn't believe my feet had ever been encumbered with such tight constraints. My escort's name was Jeskiel, and while he said it in the politest way possible, he disapproved of everything about me, which was why we stopped by the royal tailor to procure a brand-new green dress before heading to the royal stylist to have my hair and makeup done. Finally, we'd hit up the royal cobbler to get a new set of shimmering shoes that pinched in all the wrong places.

"Why wasn't what I was wearing good enough?" I asked as we finally returned to the limousine, barely able to breathe through my tight corset.

"Well, first off, your dress was fraying along the edges. Do you know what saltwater does to fabric, even in Urgu? Awful. But mostly, Queen Aine demands perfection, and will think less of you should you fail to meet her expectations."

"I suppose thank you for this torture, then."

I tried not to think about my meeting with Queen Aine and focused instead on the magnificent transformation to the Dream Realm since I last visited the Land of Oz. Gone were the horses and unicorn-pulled carriages, replaced with cars, trucks, and limousines, among other magical, previously unfathomable vehicles that ran through a series of motors and pulleys. Above us flew not only witches and birds, but planes and helicopters that allowed people to travel across Urgu in hours instead of days, even without magic.

The old town area of the Emerald City still had an air of tradition to it, and I even recognized the architecture on some of the buildings, but most of the city had been replaced with enormous towers of sleek glass and gems. The castle itself had been completely rebuilt as an enormous flawless gem of green emerald that dwarfed everything else in the city, even the Cathedral of the Six beside it.

The gates parted when we neared, and the car led us around a cobblestone circle until we reached the sleek, three-story high, metal doors, adorned with the same fairy coat of arms emblazoned on Jeskiel's tunic. I marveled at the sheer audacity of the castle. The previous bastion was a work of art, but this new one felt like it was carved from a single gem, a million carats or more. Inside, the hallways weaved in sinewy patterns, showcasing the clarity and perfection of the walls, every turn a monument to its sheer scope and splendor.

A human-sized cat with long whiskers and wearing a green robe came to greet us. "Welcome," she said. "I am Lady Lynx. It is an honor to meet you. We have so looked forward to your arrival. Has Jeskiel treated you well?"

I pressed the corset under my dress. "Oh yes. It's been quite a magical experience."

Lady Lynx smiled. "Well, you are simply a revelation."

She snapped her fingers and the doors creaked open. "Queen Aine will be very pleased."

She turned on her heels and led me through the door onto a plush purple carpet embroidered with golden fairies. In the center of the room the carpet split, one branch continuing to a similar door as the one I'd entered, the other breaking right towards a gold throne festooned with purple drapes. Lady Lynx looked as though she would continue straight and then spun quickly towards the throne. I hurried along to keep up, careful to keep my steps short to avoid tripping over the heels Jeskiel forced on me. I wasn't used to walking on dry land at all, let alone in three-inch heels.

"Your Majesty," Lady Lynx said. "Princess Ariel has made her way from the Forbidden Sea at your request."

I thought that the purple glow on the throne was an illusion of the light, but when it moved and spoke, it dawned on me why the symbol of the Emerald City's monarchy was a fairy.

"Very good, mistress," the purple light said in a scolding tone. "Leave us now."

"You have done well for yourself, Queen Aine." I curtsied as low as I could manage. "The last I heard you were leading the Unseelie fairies in the Forbidden Forest."

The purple light dimmed to reveal a fairy, no more than three apples high, floating towards me. Her skin sparkled, glistening with her every move. "I have been very blessed, your grace. I hope you approve of what we have done with the Land of Oz in your absence."

"It is lovely." I bowed my head. "Though I was never truly the ruler of this place, so you have no need of approval from me."

"I would still like it, though," Queen Aine said. "After

all, you were next in line to the throne before the coup. You were being groomed. Traitors fought wars to keep you off the throne. As I understand it, you are the last surviving soul in Urgu with any connection to Hypnos and the throne of Oz. There must be a fount of knowledge within you."

I shook my head. "I wish that were true, but I don't remember much from my time as princess."

Her face dropped. "I hope that's not true, because we desperately need your help."

"How could I possibly help you, my queen?"

"As the only monarch left alive in the entire history of the Land of Oz, or in Urgu at large, and with so many dead after the attacks by Epiales, you have unique knowledge which can help us locate a certain object kept by Nox and known to very few."

"What object is that?"

"The left eye of Rapunzel, scourge of the gods."

CHAPTER 12
CHELLE

When we blinked back into existence, we weren't on Earth anymore. The gravity pressed lighter on me, so much so that I could barely keep my feet on the ground, and the air smelled acrid. Mostly, though, it was because the technology was unlike anything I had ever seen before, except in movies. The walls, twenty-feet high, leaned together to form a triangle. Thick grooves ran along them, illuminated by different colored lights, and seemed to cut right through the steel doors my jailer led me through.

"Where are you taking me?" I growled, still struggling against its clutches.

"You are aboard the prison ship *Incarceration*."

"A bit on the nose, don't you think?"

It squeezed my arm, and I screamed out in pain. "You will learn respect before you are judged, mutant."

"Mutant?" I blurted. "I've been called a lot in my day, but that's a new one."

"We created the gorgon, and they were perfection. Then, humanity did what it always does, and infected our perfect creations."

"First," I replied, "don't put the sins of my parents on me. Second, you all created the gorgon to be beautiful sirens, until Athena got so butthurt that Poseidon defiled one of her temples by raping one of my ancestors that she cursed all of my people with hideous snakes and green skin."

My jailer scoffed. "As usual, you humans have about half the information, and you act like you know more than the gods that made you."

"Oh really? You're so smart? Then illuminate me. Where did I go wrong?"

The jailer stopped and faced me so that I could see myself reflected in its polished onyx helmet. "Poseidon did rape your ancestor, and defile my temple, but I did not curse your ancestor. I gave her the means to protect herself; magic so powerful it would ward off any attack, snakes so protective they would only let through those that wished you no harm, skin green and scaly so that none would lust after you again. I gave you the power to defend yourself because I could not defend you."

"Wait," I replied. "You said 'I'. Does that mean you are Athena?"

The voice growled, and my jailer pulled off its helmet to reveal a light-skinned woman with blue eyes and short blonde hair. I'd heard she was the most beautiful of the gods, but a scar cut across her face, splitting her nose in half, and causing her left eye to only open halfway. Her bottom lip was locked in a permanent sneer.

"I am, so please believe me when I say you are an abomination. Even before you became what you are, you were a reminder of my failure as a god."

I wanted to break my gaze, succumb to the harsh words

and become less than what I was, but I fought against my instincts and simply held her gaze.

"I've been called worse." My lip turned up in a sneer to match Athena's. "So that is why I've been captured, because I go against your perfect ideal of the universe? Because my father and mother dared to love each other?"

"Please. If I arrested every blight against the gods, I would never leave a single planet. No, you are here because Nox chose to give you life after death, which is a cardinal sin of our kind. You are to be evidence at her trial, and then you will be incinerated in the core of the universe to rid the cosmos of you."

Oh, that was all. She hated me for simply existing, but I was under arrest because Nox dared to let me be with my love again, after we had saved three realms and righted so many great wrongs. I locked my jaw.

"I will not apologize for what I am."

Athena reached a door at the front of the cabin and turned to me. "I don't expect you to. I expect you to be the proof we need to finally eliminate Nox, and then to burn alongside her as the freakshow pet that you are."

That was enough to send me into a rage, but I was on a prison ship in the middle of who-knows-where. If I wanted to survive, I needed to bide my time to take my shot at the appropriate time. Athena would pay. That much was assured, but I would likely only get one shot to take her down. I needed to take it wisely.

She led me through the rest of the ship, each room looking remarkably similar to the next. In some, robots went about making repairs or working on computers, but they all had the same basic structure.

"Don't you get bored looking at this every day?"

"I do not get the luxury of boredom," she replied. I felt the anger in her words. "I have a job to do."

She pulled me through another door, and a dozen animals and human voices hollered out to me. "A job? Aren't you a god? All the gods I've met have been shiftless lay-abouts."

"Some of my brothers and sisters have that luxury. Others of us actually want the universe to remain intact. Hard as it might be for you to believe, there are thousands of things that must be done to keep the universe spinning, and many of us take that responsibility seriously."

The screams were louder through the next door, a room filled with cages and jail cells containing all manner of magical beings, from hairy birds with beaks sticking out from their cells to giant, skinless bears that roared as we passed, and to filthy humans wearing tattered clothes that they pulled tight around them.

Athena finally stopped at a dank metal cell and threw me inside, locking the door. She gave me one last mean mug before storming off.

"Chelle?" a familiar voice said from across the cell block. A shaky figure appeared, and even through the bars, I knew it was Nox. The goddess of darkness, and the one responsible for my current plight. She looked like a shell of her former self.

CHAPTER 13

RED

"Do you know what it means to be virtuous?" Rama asked as he walked me back to the bar. All eyes were on him, and every mouth went agape, and yet, he kept his eyes forward. Every man and woman there wanted to be him and be with him. A sly smirk told me he loved the attention, was desperate for it even, but he couldn't show it. That would be undignified.

"To be a good person," I replied. "That's what I always thought."

"Well, I am not a person, but I consider myself virtuous. Some have even called me the god of virtue, but they get it all wrong. Philosophers say that it is about having high moral standards, but everyone assigns their own morals to their ideals of virtue, depending on the civilization and context. A hero to one group is a villain to others, and while one person thinks you have high moral character, another will think you are devoid of it."

"I really don't need a morality lesson today," I said. "I just need your paramour's address so I can get this stupid bow for you."

He laughed. "She's not my paramour, and if I knew her address, then I would go over there myself. No, I'm afraid you will have to be resourceful to find Kadlu's location."

"Of course. And here I thought you might help me."

"What I have to give is some of the most powerful information in the whole universe. That kind of information doesn't come easy." He pushed the elevator button for me. "And now, I must apologize."

"It's fine." I shook my head. "I guess I shouldn't have expected you to help me."

"No," he said. "That's not why. It's because at the bottom of this elevator there's a squad of elite soldiers waiting to take you to the Celestial Realm for trial."

"You set me up."

"Not exactly." He held up his hands. "I know you think that I have lied to you, and you feel betrayed. Just remember that virtue is different to everyone, and I am following mine, and my loyalty, to my people." The door slid open, and he pushed me inside. "If you do happen to survive them, come back and I will bring you into my confidence."

I snarled at him. "If I see you again, I'll kill you."

The door closed. "You can certainly try."

I had about five seconds before I was swarmed with soldiers. I leapt onto the walls and smashed my hand against the metal escape hatch on top of the elevator. The latch flew open, and wind swirled in. The top of the hub was three hundred stories high, and the elevator made the trip in five seconds, so it was going at quite a clip, but compared to a squad of soldiers, gravity seemed like a piece of cake.

I flipped my legs into the newly-opened hole and pulled myself up just as the elevator arrived at the lobby. The elevator to the rooftop bar had no other stops, which meant I either needed to climb up 3,000 feet into the air or take out a squad of well-trained soldiers working for the gods themselves. If I climbed, best case scenario I would make it up to the roof and be caught by Rama. I had no choice but to fight.

"Halt!" a robotic voice shouted when the door opened. "You're under—where is she?"

Two soldiers, dressed completely in black from their polished helmets to their gloves, rushed into the elevator holding thick, fat guns with glowing orange barrels.

"I don't see her in here. Maybe our intel was—" One of them looked up at the open hatch and that's when I attacked. I wasn't going to get a better chance. I leapt down into the elevator and wrapped my legs around one of the soldier's necks, snapping it. I swiped their gun before they collapsed on the ground.

Three more soldiers waited for me in the doorway. I rolled behind the other soldier in the elevator and grabbed them around the neck, sticking the gun to their temple.

"Tell them to put the gun down, or I'll shoot you."

The soldier stammered for a second, then found their resolve. "Shoot her!"

I kicked the soldier out of the elevator and leapt up to the ceiling as laser beams tore them to shreds. When the lasers died down, I jumped down and fired, taking out one of the soldiers with two shots to the chest. I cracked the second with the butt of the gun and they fell to the ground. The final soldier fired, and I dodged behind a column that the lasers obliterated. I tumbled away and pulled the trigger, cutting my adversary in half.

With the soldiers subdued, the firing stopped, and an eerie calm came over the lobby. I searched their pockets, coming up with several energy cartridges, a pair of laser-tipped knives that I stuffed in my pockets, and a thermal grenade. Between all of them was several hundred dollars in local currency, which would be a boon since I had no idea where to go now, but it definitely involved being on this planet longer than I liked.

My search through the soldier's remains was cut short as a spotlight shone through the glass walls of the entrance. Another squad of soldiers descended from a hover truck, and I sprinted through the back of the building, leaving Rama to explain my mess to his snooty worshippers. I almost wished I could see his face when he found out I escaped.

Almost as much as I wanted to kill the jerk.

CHAPTER 14
ROSE

"What do you mean you can't find her?" I said. "The only thing I ever asked of you was to keep the two of us safe. If you can't even do that, then what was all this for?"

After finding Chelle missing, I called in my team, who called in another team, who called in yet another team. A dozen FBI agents had converged on my apartment, combing through every inch of it. Cheyenne didn't like it, and I had to pick her up into my arms. Even with me cradling her like a baby, she wouldn't stop barking.

Agent Edwards tipped his glasses down, revealing a pair of emerald-green eyes that I couldn't believe he kept hidden. "If you remember, we told you not to move into a hundred-year-old building filled with nooks and crannies, but you insisted on having some semblance of a normal life, so this is at least as much on you as on us."

"Do you really think this is the appropriate time to throw that in my face?" I snapped. Cheyenne barked at him. "Good girl."

"No," he said. "It's not. Sorry."

"That's better," I replied. "Now, explain to me how you lost my fiancée."

"Fiancée?" Agent Edwards's voice had a hint of excitement. "Congratulations."

"Thank you." I bit my lip. "That doesn't answer my question."

"Because we don't know," a nasally voice said from the couch. The man stood up and pressed his comically large glasses back on his nose. "If you remember, a condition of your enrollment in our protection program was to implant a small GPS device under your skin." He touched my forearm right under the elbow. "Right there."

"Yeah, I remember," I said, rubbing it. "Also, don't touch me."

"Sorry." He turned to pull his computer from the glass coffee table that he was smudging with his greasy hands. He turned the screen to me, and it showed a map with a red blip pinging in its center. "That's you. There should be another ping for Chelle, but no matter what we run in our program—she's gone."

"So, somebody disabled the tracker before they kidnapped her? Who would do that?"

He shrugged. "We don't know. Very few people even know about the trackers, and the technology is state of the art. They are only something we use in high priority cases."

"Do you think it was an inside job, then?" I asked.

Agent Edwards pressed his glasses back, hiding his green eyes once again. "We're looking into every possibility. It's not like she just disappeared off the face of the planet."

"Right," I said, except I wasn't so sure. I had known some crazy stuff in my life, and while the FBI was pretty much clueless about exactly what magic could do, I knew better than just about anyone how magic could literally make you disappear off the face of the planet. Maybe she was taken off world.

I excused myself to the bathroom and slid the door closed. The magical world almost universally hated me, that much was clear, but I needed them now. The FBI would not like this next part, but if they couldn't help me locate Chelle immediately, I needed to expand my search beyond their capabilities. While they investigated the terrestrial side of her disappearance, I would work on the magical side of things. Perhaps bringing in an expert could help. Of course, my list of magical contacts in the world was woefully short.

I closed my eyes and waved my hand over my forearm. "*Lorem perdere intus peregrinorum.*" The small 'pop' hopefully meant the tracker disappeared into the body of a rat ten stories underground. Cheyenne barked at my feet, and I picked her up. "You're going to hate this, but with you there at least somebody will be on my side." I sighed loudly and placed my free hand on my chest. "*Detrahet me in Jamil.*"

The room crackled, and then everything fell dark. When the world came back into view, I was in the center of my old college, with every eye in a hundred yards focused on me, human and magical beings alike. I looked for Jamil in the crowd. Cheyenne growled at everyone that eyed me but didn't leave the comfort of my arms.

"What do you want?" The voice startled me. When I turned, Jamil looked back at me in her wood nymph form, the one she'd kept hidden under an amulet the last time I saw her.

"You look good," I replied, but Cheyenne wasn't so sure. She readied herself to pounce. "This is a good look on you."

"Something I would have liked to decide on my own, but after your latest stunt at the Spindle, my amulet stopped working, and suddenly, everybody knew who I was anyway."

"No, that wasn't me—" A thought occurred to me. "Etsop died before that battle. Maybe with his death his magic fell."

She shook her head. "You don't get it. The amulet was built on secrecy magic. Once you revealed us to the world, there was nothing to bind it together."

I placed my hand to my face. "I'm so sorry. I didn't mean to—"

"No, you never mean to do anything, do you? You just barrel forward without thinking and expect people to forgive you when they become an unintended consequence of your selfishness."

She began crying in the middle of her speech, and the tears fell from my eyes as well.

"Feel better?" I asked, choking back my sadness.

"Yeah," she replied with a sigh. "I've been waiting to say that to you forever."

"I'll be the villain of your story if that helps you. You wouldn't be the first and definitely won't be the last. I was hoping that maybe with everything we've been through, at least you would know my heart was in the right place."

"I know that," Jamil said. "It doesn't make it any less frustrating, but I've said my piece. Now, say yours."

"I feel even worse now to ask, but—I need your help."

She laughed. "Of course you do. Why would you ever come to say hi? You haven't called to check in once since you left, did you know that?"

"Yeah, I did." I stared at my feet. "I thought you might hate me, and I couldn't stand the thought, so I stayed away. Seems like I was right."

Jamil touched my shoulder. "I don't hate you. I don't

much like you right now, but I never thought I would be able to walk freely as myself, and I have you to thank for that." She stared hard into my eyes. "In a way, I guess I owe you, so what stupid thing do you need my help with?"

"Chelle is missing. The CIA thinks that she's been kidnapped, and her tracker was disabled, but my gut says this is something magic. I was hoping you might know somebody who can tell me if Chelle vanished from Earth, if she's de—what happened to her."

Jamil growled. "I was all ready to say no to you, but then you brought Chelle into this. I still like her."

"So you'll help me?"

"Yes." She looked around, and suddenly I realized there were hundreds of students circling around us, including plenty of magical beings like Jamil that Cheyenne started to bark at. "Maybe we should go somewhere more private, though."

"I think that would be wise. Usually when this many people gather around me, it's because they want to cause me bodily harm."

CHAPTER 15
NIMUE

I thought the Faceless Woman's forest was disgusting, but it was a regular resort compared to the rest of the countryside. No sun shone in the gloomy abyss, and yet I could make out everything on the Dark Planet, as if the Faceless Woman gave me sight to see, even though she couldn't... yet. Microscopic lights rose from the flowers and the small animals carried a spark of life inside them, helping illuminate the desolate and burnt land.

My stomach churned while I continued towards the town where Cassandra Vespertine waited to lead me to the capitol. Tentacled monsters with glowing eyes stared at me from beneath the clay. The ground undulated and I lost my footing every few hundred feet, as my eyes tracked the monstrous horrors loping across the horizon.

One of the creatures was as tall as the tallest tree at the edge of the forest, with three long legs and a cloud of black ichor for a body. A giant ball of eyeballs contained in squishy flesh left a trail of slime behind it. If these were the monsters out in the open, I couldn't imagine what kind of nightmare beings hid in the world's dark crevices. I kept a close eye out for something unimaginable coming to destroy me, but also secretly hoped that something would try to take me down.

After all, the last time I navigated a plane of pure horrors, in the Nightmare Realm, I was without powers, and I still survived. This place was exponentially worse, filled with beings that would be rejected even from Epiales's domain for being too twisted, but now I had magic, and part of me ached to use it.

I expected some sort of humanoid sentience working the stores when I finally reached the town. What I saw instead were smaller creatures that, compared to the ones outside the city, were barely scary at all. A being with arms twice the length of their torso worked a forge in the blacksmith shop. A single eyeball with ten tentacles cut meat in a butcher shop, and a bear that had been split in half from nape to navel worked forging a sword in an armory.

"Are you her?" a raspy voice said from a house on the far edge of town. "Rapunzel's girl?"

"Who?" I asked, walking closer.

"Oh yes, I forgot. She does not go by that name anymore. I have known her since the beginning." A woman stepped out of the door—or, what remained of a woman after all her skin had been flayed. Her eyes were black, and her mouth cracked. A circle with a slash through it had been carved on her head, and her hair was black as her eyes. "I am Cassandra. Rapu—the Faceless Woman told me of your arrival. I expected you sooner."

She held out her hand, though I was trepidatious to take it. Her muscles tensed at my touch.

I grimaced. "Charmed, I'm sure."

"You are new here. I can tell it in your eyes when you

look at me. Trust me, I am not the most horrific thing on this cursed planet."

"I believe you," I replied. "I have already seen worse in my travels."

She beckoned me inside. "Can I get you anything? Tea, maybe?"

I hadn't had tea in a long time, but I couldn't imagine they brewed anything like I remembered. "What kind is it?"

Her home was small and plain, furnished with a wood-fire stove, a small bed, and a table with two warped chairs. She shuffled over to the stove and flicked her finger to start the fire. "It's not all that bad, but we get no sun on this planet, so we can grow little except that which thrives in the darkness. The mushrooms that grow on the base of some of our trees make a decent brew."

"I think I'll pass," I said, trying to hide my grimace. "Thanks for the offer."

She shrugged. "Probably for the best. Who knows what it would do to your mortal body? It might paralyze you or turn you into a monster like the rest of us."

I knew the polite thing to say was that she wasn't horrific, but my mouth couldn't say the words. Instead, I bowed my head. "Thank you for the offer. I think we should just take care of the matter at hand."

"Patience, young one." Her voice was raspier than before. "All in time."

I pulled a face. "I'm not young. This body is young, but I am hundreds of years old."

"My apologies. I did not realize." She poured hot water into a cup. "I would give anything for young skin again. Do you know what it is like to live in agony at your every movement for generations on end?"

"No, I don't. It must have been terrible."

"It was." She touched the mark on her forehead. "If not for Rapunzel, I would never have felt any relief."

"Who did that to you? Was it Hastur?"

"Yes." She took her tea and brought it to the table, where we sat next to each other. "They call him the King in Yellow. The gods appointed him to this post looking over the worst of their creations, but even for this place, he is twisted."

"What did you do to displease him so?"

"I refused to sleep with him, if you can even call it that." She sucked her teeth. "There was a time when this was a normal planet, you know. Before we became a prison for the god's misadventures; before they threw us into our own dimension and left us to fend for ourselves. Everyone I love is dead, a victim of either the King in Yellow, or these horrors the gods created. Only I live, as punishment for betraying his every whim."

"I'm sorry that happened to you." I swallowed hard. "I can see why you want to take him down."

"It will not solve everything," she replied. "But with the king dead, much of his twisted magic will stop, and the world can heal."

"Will you die?" I asked. "When he dies?"

"Gods, I hope so." She took another sip of tea. "But let us rest for a minute. There is plenty of time for plotting once I am done with my tea."

"Very well." I nodded. "You know, I think I will try a cup."

The woman smiled. "It is an acquired taste, but its bitterness will prepare you for the journey ahead."

CHAPTER 16
ARIEL

"What are you talking about?" I asked, giving Queen Aine a baffled look. "I have no idea who that is. And why would you want her eye?"

It clearly wasn't the answer Queen Aine wanted, and her face fell. Well, it didn't quite fall so much as undulate up and down, alternating between confusion, frustration, consternation, and anger.

"What do you mean you don't know what I'm talking about?" she finally said through tiny, gritted fairy teeth.

"Exactly what I said. I've never heard of Rapunzel, and I have no idea where her left eye would be. I suggest you look at her face. That's where eyes usually go, unless she was dusted, of course." I stopped for a second, waiting for it to land before I continued. "Can I go now?"

"No, you cannot go!" Queen Aine's voice squeaked in frustration, and she took a moment to compose herself. "I don't understand. We talked to the Fates—to Hypnos—and they all said you would know where to find the missing eye."

"Why don't you just ask Nox?"

"She has vanished, and we have as of yet not been able to track her down."

"Oh right." I rolled my eyes. "Duh. That's why I'm here."

"Verily." She pressed her fingers to the bridge of her nose. "You need to come with me."

I wanted to protest, but Ursula had asked me to be helpful. Because I am forever a dutiful daughter, I followed Queen Aine through various rooms and hallways until two guards opened a pair of metal doors that led us to the palace grounds. The walkway outside the castle was filled with pilgrims waiting to speak to the Fates, just as I had during my day, praying for a way home or some other favor that would allow them to get back into the world.

"That is quite a line," I said as we headed towards the Rainbow Bridge separating the Emerald City from the island that houses the Obsidian Spindle.

"They are insistent on seeing the Fates, but the Fates cannot see anyone without Chelle here. She seems to have disappeared off the face of the universe."

"I don't understand," I said. "Who is Chelle? What of Clotho, Lachesis, and Atropos?"

"Atropos died during the great war," Queen Aine said. "Chelle took her place, but then Nox gave her the freedom to leave the Dream Realm. We haven't seen her since, which means all these poor souls are out of luck. They just either don't know it yet or refuse to accept it."

"This Chelle...she was allowed to leave the Dream Realm even after dying?" I asked. "How is that possible? I have always been told it was impossible to do such a thing."

"Don't ask me. I know magic, but what the gods can do is lost on me."

Nox told me when she brought me to Ursula that it was the only safe place in the Dream Realm. Had she been able to bring me back to Earth this whole time? Had she lied to me the hundreds of times I asked for her help? Queen Aine didn't seem like the right person to ask about such things. She was clearly as clueless as I was, even if she wore a crown.

"MOVE!" Queen Aine screamed. She pressed her hands outwards, creating a small wave of force that fashioned a path between the horde of people. They tumbled over each other towards the edges of the bridge.

Queen Aine continued past a small battalion of guards separating the Obsidian Spindle's entrance from the throngs of people. The door opened when she knocked, causing groans and complaints from the crowd.

"Tough luck," she grumbled. "Access is one of the few benefits of leadership."

I hadn't seen the inside of the Spindle since I ducked below the surface, and it was as plain and non-descript as I remembered. I thought that there would be magic in every inch of the place for such a holy site, but it was just a black stone tower, dank and musty, with a thousand steps between us and the lair of the Fates.

Queen Aine didn't go up the stairs. Instead, she walked to a pair of doors and pushed a button on the wall beside them. After a few seconds, a bell dinged, and the doors opened. She fluttered inside and pushed a button.

"Let's go," Queen Aine said. "It's several hundred floors down."

"Down?" I frowned. "We're not going up?"

"Not if you want to talk to the Fates. They live in the Heart of Urgu now. If you want to see them, we have to take the elevator."

I stepped inside with her and marveled as the elevator jerked, leading us down rapidly into the heart of the planet.

When the doors opened again, we entered a cavern alit with the pink light from the dreams of millions, distilled into the orbs we used as currency and power.

"Do keep up," Queen Aine said, continuing through the enormous cavern. She mumbled an incantation when she reached a small door, and the metal snakes surrounding it clasped together to unlock it.

We continued down a small corridor, her flying and me walking, until it broke open into a sight I never thought I would see again. The Heart of Urgu, a giant crystal containing the souls of all the Dreamers asleep right now, depositing their spark of the divine before it manifested in the form of the dream orbs.

Everything in the room throbbed in time with the Heart, which let out a tender pulse every second. Two cots had been built next to it, and two old gorgons knelt in prayer.

"We didn't think you would get here yet," Lachesis said with a grumble.

"Everything has been off since Chelle left," Clotho added, opening her eyes. "Let me get a look at you, child."

"Tell her what you told me," Queen Aine said.

Clotho and Lachesis looked at each other, then Lachesis turned to me. "We see the Dream Realm falling into darkness if the left eye is not found. The entirety of the Dream Realm, maybe the universe, rests on locating it."

"So you see," Queen Aine said. "We need to know what you know."

"I'm sorry," I said. "I wish I could help you, but I have no idea what you're talking about."

They each put a hand on my face. Their brows furrowed and their eyes found each other.

Lachesis sighed. "This is very disappointing."

"Your memories have been tainted, my dear." Clotho shook her head. "Written and rewritten a thousand times. I'm not sure what we need is still buried under there." She tapped my cheek softly. "Truly a tragedy, for all of us."

What were they talking about? My memories, tainted?

"But I remember you, and I remember the Emerald City. How could those memories remain while others are locked away?"

"It is powerful, old, precise magic," Lachesis said. "Without our third, we are powerless to recover them, but you must, or all hope is lost."

CHAPTER 17

ROSE

I left New York without so much as a goodbye, let alone a leash for Cheyenne, so Jamil begrudgingly stopped by a pet store so I could buy one, along with some treats and a little doggy carrier.

"You're sure she's not going to piss in my car?" Jamil asked when we got back on the road. She had upgraded her wheels since the last time I saw her, and now drove a leather-seated SUV.

Cheyenne sat cautiously but patiently on my lap in the passenger's seat as I pet her. "Oh yes, she's potty trained and everything. She just doesn't like people, or magical beings, or other dogs, and she has crippling anxiety. Honestly, she's a mess." I bent down and spoke to her like a puppy. "But we love her so much, don't we?"

"Ew," Jamil replied. "I hate 'baby voice'."

"It's statistically proven that doggos like it better when you speak to them like that." I said all of that in the same baby voice, directed soothingly at Cheyenne. "So, eat butts, or whatever."

"Just leave her in the car when we get to Lenny's. He doesn't like dogs."

"I am not leaving her in a car! It's like, 100 degrees out there. Do you know how hot it will be in this car? She'll die."

"It'll just be a couple of minutes. Do you want to get your girlfriend back or not?"

"Hello," I held up my ring. "Fiancée."

"Did she actually propose?" Jamil asked. "Because you told me she left before she proposed."

"Whatever. Same difference. I said yes."

"To a box," Jamil said. "It's not the same thing."

"Well, when you have somebody that loves you enough to buy a ring, and then disappears on you without notice, then you can decide how to deal with it. Right now, I need to call Chelle my fiancée, and I need Cheyenne around. She's my emotional support doggo."

"Who is also a possessive, anxiety-ridden wreck."

"You don't need to be well-adjusted to help somebody else. Have you ever met a psychologist? They're all bananas, and they still help lots of people." I bent down to Cheyenne. "Just like she helps me, don't you, girl?" She licked the tip of my nose. "Thank you for the kisses."

"Disgusting." Jamil gripped the steering wheel tighter. "You know she licks her butt with that tongue, right?"

"I don't care."

We took the 5 south for about an hour, and then turned onto a road that seemed to lead nowhere fast. We passed several houses on big plots of land before we reached a big white house. Based on how badly the paint was chipped, I guessed it hadn't been touched up for several decades.

"Lenny doesn't like gods," Jamil said. "And he hates

you, but he's the best person I know for figuring out what's going on."

"Why is that?" I asked, holding Cheyenne in my arms as I got out of the car.

"Because he's paranoid as hell, which means even though he hates us, he knows everything about us."

Jamil used the golden sheep knocker on the black door. Nothing happened for a long while, then finally footsteps approached. I saw the top of Lenny's head through the square windowpane above the knocker. He didn't have much hair left, and that which he did decided to violently rebel against the rest of his body by flailing every which way.

"Who is it?"

"It's me, Lenny. Open up."

"I hate when people do that," he mumbled with his grating voice. "Do you know how many people I meet in a given week? You can't just say 'it's me.' You're not my mother."

"No," Jamil said. "Mostly because I have better taste than to bang a god, though."

"Wait, he's a demigod?" I whispered.

Before she could answer, the door swung open and a pasty man with a beer gut stood in the threshold. He wasn't wearing much besides a pair of boxers with monkeys on them and a cotton robe that had "Holiday Inn" emblazoned across the left breast. He smoked a cigarette, and it wasn't his first of the day given the plume of smoke that made its escape as he stood bow-legged in the doorway.

"Yes, that's right. I'm a demigod." He stuck his cigarette in his mouth and held out his arms wide. "Behold my glory."

I had met a lot of gods, and while they weren't all in

peak physical condition, they all had a certain way about them…a class that Lenny absolutely didn't possess. He was, in all ways, absolutely average, maybe even slightly below.

"Yes, you're wonderful," Jamil said flatly. "Can we come inside?"

Lenny opened his mouth to speak, but Cheyenne yipped at him, trying to lunge out of the carrier to attack. "Get that thing back!" he cried. "Jesus, Jamil. I thought I told you how much I hate dogs."

"That's barely a dog, Lenny. And barking at you shows she has good judgment."

I stepped away and patted Cheyenne, trying to soothe her. "I'm sorry about that. She's not the best around new people, or old people."

"Then why did you bring her to a new person's house? Just to scare the piss out of them?"

"Her girlfriend's gone," Jamil said, returning his glare. "You know a lot about this stuff, so I thought you could help us."

"I absolutely can help you, but why would I?" He pointed his crooked finger at me. "Do you know what a storm of crap you've kicked up in the past couple months, girl?"

I nodded. "I have some idea, but I couldn't help it. Nimue was going to open the Obsidian Spindle and destroy everything."

"I don't care one bit about that battle. It's everything that's come after it that makes me hate you."

"Hey!' Jamil snapped. "That's my friend. I hate what she's done, too, don't get me wrong, but nobody talks to her that way except me."

"I'm sorry," I said, Cheyenne having calmed down. "It was the only way the government would protect me. They told me it would be a good thing, to tell people about magical beings, that it would help us all heal, and bond."

"Yes," Lenny groaned. "How well did that work for the X-Men?"

"Poorly," Jamil said. "And somehow this went worse."

"Look, I can't change the past." I set Cheyenne on the ground, and she hid behind my legs. "If I could, I would, I swear I would, but my fiancée is missing, and Jamil says you can help. I'm desperate. I'll give anything to get Chelle back."

"Anything?" Lenny said. "Okay, let me kill the dog."

"Never!" I shouted, snatching Cheyenne up and holding her away from the brute. "How dare you—"

"Hey!" Lenny said. "You said anything, and I had to know your line."

I pet Cheyenne. "Don't listen to the bad man. I won't let anything happen to you." I turned my eyes up to him. "Anything else."

"If you're so close with the government, then why don't you get them to help you?"

"I tried, but they aren't much help with magical things."

Lenny snorted. "That's an understatement." His eyes narrowed. "Okay, I'll help you, under one condition."

"Anything, except killing my dog...or Chelle," I added at the last second. "Or Jamil."

"Nothing like that." He stepped out of the house, the sun bearing down on his white chest. "You promise me you'll never do another interview on camera, for the rest of your life, and I'll do it."

"That's a condition of the FBI protecting me."

"Then I guess you're going to have to find some other

type of protection. You're a big girl, though. I'm sure you'll figure it out...or you can find somebody else to help you."

I sighed. What good was being alive without Chelle? "Fine, I promise."

He held out his hand. "Shake on it."

Cheyenne did not like me moving towards Lenny, and made her hatred known by baring her teeth and barking until I had no choice but to tie her to the pole at the end of the porch. She still screamed bloody murder, though, and she was right to do so. My hackles were raised, just like hers, but there was no other choice.

I pressed my hand into Lenny's and let the gooey slime of his sweat coat my palm. "There you go."

"Swear it," he growled.

"Is this necessary?" Jamil said.

Lenny grinned wide and sloppy, revealing his baked bean teeth. "Only if she wants my help."

"Fine," I said. "I swear that I'll never do another interview about magical beings ever again."

"And in exchange, I'll help you find your paramour."

Blue light shot from our palms and tightened around our arms until I winced in pain. The light dug into my arms and then disappeared. He didn't have to tell me what had just happened. I knew a fairy contract when I saw one. If I broke it, my heart would stop, and I would die.

"Pleasure doing business with you," he said. "Now, let's go inside and talk specifics."

"I'm not leaving her outside," I said.

His eyes narrowed. "Fine then. I'll bring some lemonade out back...and some water for your stupid mutt."

"Can we just go already?" I asked. "We're kind of in a rush."

"We'll go find your little girlfriend," Lenny said. "But after lemonade. I can't think without a sugar rush."

Jamil rolled her eyes. "Just go along with it. I'll rush him, and we'll be back in New York within the hour. I promise."

"Whatever," I spat. "This better be worth it."

CHAPTER 18

RED

I didn't know whether to kill Rama for turning me in or thank him for giving me the heads up that I was about to be captured. *Wait.* Why would he turn me in and then help me escape? It didn't make any sense. Of course, gods were always doing things that didn't make sense. If I got out of this situation, I would take him up on his offer and return to interrogate him about it.

The spotlight from the hover jet that had been tracking me for miles shined on me, and I had to move again. No time for thinking about whether Rama saved me or betrayed me. I was much more interested in surviving.

The hover jet beelined towards me. Out of each side, two soldiers leapt in flying suits and aimed themselves towards me.

"Resistance is unacceptable. You are putting all of these lives at risk!" The pilot of the hover jet shouted at me with the craft's megaphone every time they caught up to me. No way could I give up now. I'd killed too many of them. There was no chance they would be lenient.

I didn't want to run, and I didn't want to give myself up. I wanted to end this and show these creeps not to mess with me. I had no idea what I'd done to warrant such a vicious response, but if the gods were really after me, then I needed them to know that I was more trouble than I was worth.

The lasers peppered the street as I rushed past innocent, clueless civilians. In the next instant, they were dead. I grabbed one of the knives from my side and flipped it at one of the flying soldiers. I wasn't used to using it, so it missed the soldier's head. It still cut their arm, causing them to lose altitude and crash into the side of a building.

Three left—and the big hover jet, of course. I had already cut down two dozen of the soldiers. How many could fit in a twenty-foot-long ship? They had to be running out of men. I would teach them to underestimate me. I refilled the charge on my laser gun, spun around, and pulled down two more of the soldiers when I sliced through their hands and arms, knocking them to the ground.

I looked back and smiled. I had been leading them across the city, looking for a suitable building to scale. It had to be a valuable one, one that they'd be hesitant to fire upon. The ancillary nodes of the network were not as important as the central one, but if you destroyed one it would cut off power to a good chunk of Chippara, from hospitals to hotels and even things that didn't start with an H.

The hover jet was powerful, but it hadn't fired at me yet, instead sending out its little soldiers to do the job but doing its best not to lose sight of me. I turned down an alley and swerved right and left until I reached the end of a blind alley. I leapt onto the wall and waited until the soldier in the flying suit turned the corner, then kicked him right in the face. He crashed into the wall and slumped over, unconscious.

If my plan was going to work, I needed his suit. I didn't know how it worked, but all it had to do was help me glide, just like the flying squirrel suits back on Earth. I tore the suit off him and slipped it on just as the hover jet appeared above me. I smiled at the pilot before latching onto the wall and pulling myself to the roof. I rushed along the top of the building, leaping to the next roof, and then the next.

If the hover jet fired the cannons on either side of their wings, I could be toasted, but not without leveling a whole city block. The pilot couldn't afford to do that, at least not so close to the node.

Or at least that was what I hoped was the case as I leapt onto the edge of the node and began to climb. The side of the building was slippery, but the edges gave enough of a foothold that I could climb quickly, until I was nose to nose with the hover jet.

"Surrender now," the pilot shouted into the bullhorn. "Or we will blow you out of the air."

"I don't think you will!" I screamed back. I looked back and saw that I was just slightly above the jet. I jumped, holding out my arms as I glided towards the aircraft. When I was close enough, I took out the thermal grenade and pulled the pin, dropping it into the huge fans that allowed the jet to hover.

There was a look of horror on the pilot's face as I flew past, after his realization of what I'd done but before the explosion. I almost felt sorry for him, but it was not my fault he was trying to kill me.

I extended my arms as the explosion propelled me

forward, looking back in time to see the hover jet crash into the node. The lights flickered and then a quarter of the city fell into darkness.

CHAPTER 19

CHELLE

"They're moving again," Nox said, matter-of-factly.

My stomach lurched, and a loud hum squeaked through the jail cell. "Don't talk to me."

"I know you hate me, and you have every reason to."

"You're damn right I do," I shot back. "I was perfectly happy with my life in Urgu."

"That's not true and you know it," Nox replied. "You were desperate to get back to Rose, and I made it happen. Let's not pretend this was all me acting against your will."

"At least then I wouldn't have been arrested by the gods for crimes I had absolutely nothing to do with."

"Piffle." She leaned her elbows against the cell bars. "If you can look me in the eyes and tell me you would trade the months you had with her, even if they are the last you ever get, then I will listen to you complain for the rest of this trip. It's not like everyone doesn't blame me for everything, anyway. But if you can't, then please, kindly shut up."

I wanted to shout at her, but she was right. Having those three months with Rose, where I could hear her heartbeat in her chest, and feel her lips when she kissed me, was everything. "You're right. I loved my time with her." I leaned my head back and sighed. "But now I'm a fugitive for simply being alive."

"For that, I am truly sorry," Nox tsked. "I knew the risks of creating you, but—well, I simply hate everything about how the gods run things, and I suppose this allowed me my little rebellion. Look what it has gotten me."

"Then you knew it was wrong?"

"Of course I knew it was wrong," she said, shooting me a look. "I wrote most of those stupid rules myself back before the Board was formed. That doesn't make them any less horrible." She sighed. "What we did...in the beginning, it was good. We were doing good, but just like anything, power corrupted us. You couldn't even see the corruption unless you were looking hard for it. Zeus twisted a rule here, Brahma messed with something there, Svarog rewrote a dogma there. It was all very innocent, or that's how it looked from the outside. People would complain sporadically, but there was always some god to defend it and give examples of why the rules needed to change with the times. By the time I knew how messed up everything had gotten, it was too late."

"Why didn't you do anything about it?"

"I did!" Nox lifted her head to the ceiling. "Or at least I tried. You cannot go against the Pantheon, even if you were there from the beginning. Once the Board took over the United Federation of Gods, it was too powerful to stop. So, I retreated into the background, into the Dream Realm, into the shadows, biding my time."

"And where do I fit into your plan?"

"You don't," she said. "You were just a nice thing I was trying to do to prove the gods aren't all bad."

"Who were you trying to prove this to? Me?"

She shook her head. "No, to myself." She turned towards her wall. "I'm sorry for involving you in this, but make no mistake, you are part of this now, for better or worse."

"Worse, definitely for worse."

"We'll see. There are plenty of games left to play. I hope, for both of our sakes, you are wrong. After all, things often look darkest before the dawn."

"That's not true," I said. "It's darkest way before sunrise, when the sun is furthest from the sun. You literally made the stars. How can you not know how they work?"

Nox rolled her eyes. "It's just an expression. How about this? You must travel through the dark to get to the light, and often, things get much darker before they get lighter." She spun back to me. "See? That's a mouthful, which is why I didn't say it."

"Fair enough," I replied. "I still don't like you, though."

"Join the club."

CHAPTER 20

NIMUE

The flayed woman, Cassandra Vespertine, went about procuring our passage to the capital while I waited for her to return. It wasn't anything personal, she told me, but I was a freak of nature, having no defects or flaws to speak of, and I would disturb the others, not to mention cause tongues to wag. Imagine me being the oddity in a town full of them.

After several hours waiting in her tiny thatch house, devoid of anything to read or watch, I stood up when Cassandra finally hurried through the door without an apology for taking so long. I opened my mouth to chew her out for the indignity of being forced to wait, but she raised her finger to stay my voice.

She picked up a small bag and turned back to the door. "Come with me," was all she said.

"Where are we going?" I asked when we were storming across the village. The eyes of the horrific villagers found me and wouldn't let go as I passed. Even after I was out of their line of sight, they poked their heads—those that had proper heads—out their doors and windows to track me into the distance.

"You can't go to the capital looking like that. It's unseemly. Just look at how everyone is looking at you."

"Maybe they're just entranced by my beauty," I said, sticking my nose high into the air.

"No, that's not it. Horrified by it, maybe." She peered at my face. "If the king sees you like that, he will turn you inside out. Is that what you want?"

"No."

She nodded curtly. "I didn't think so. Luckily, I have a friend who can help."

I didn't like the sound of that, but I promised myself I would do anything to learn the secrets of the Faceless Woman's power, to stand next to the gods and make them tremble. To do that, I needed the piece of the Faceless Woman's body the king kept around his neck.

"No other questions?" Cassandra turned on her heels. "Then let us continue."

The small town was surrounded by a collection of knobby trees. Not nearly enough to call it a forest, but thick enough to hide a small hut. The hut was nothing special, smaller even than the houses in Cassandra's town and more run down, which was saying something. When we were a hundred or so feet away, the skinned woman stuck out her arm and pressed it against my chest.

"Don't move."

A shiver went up my spine. I had dealt with my share of horrific things in my day but feeling the undulating pulses of Cassandra's muscle was excessive, even for me, and I leapt back from her.

"Baba," she called out. "I've returned to honor your half of our agreement."

The ground shook under our feet as several dozen stakes poked out of the ground, waist high, topped with glowing skulls. They snaked around the grounds up to the hut's door, and Cassandra followed them closely.

"The path changes all the time. If you step outside of it, you become her property, and you certainly don't want her to get control of your pretty face."

I touched my cheek involuntarily. "But isn't that exactly what you're planning to do?"

"Yes, but on our terms, not hers." She turned to me. "In order to entreat with Baba, you must be willing to make a deal—one which you must complete exactly as she specifies, or she will take control of your soul."

"And you made this deal with her?" I asked.

She nodded. "It's easy when your aims are aligned. She agreed to help us in exchange for the throne of the king when we kill him."

I couldn't help but smile. "A woman after my own heart."

"Do not mistake that she is a woman or has a heart. Baba is a feral beast, older than the hills, and bound here when this planet was young. The gods fear her nearly as much as they do Rapunzel. If you value your freedom, speak carefully when you meet her and keep your words brief, or she will twist them and use them against you."

I had other questions, but we reached the rotten wooden door before I could speak up. It creaked open for us to enter.

CHAPTER 21

RED

I snaked my way back around the darkened section of the city to the central hub of Chippara, taking advantage of the shadows at every opportunity. The light from the hover jet explosion dimmed quickly and I exited the area before the police arrived on the scene. Still, the smoke rose high into the air, backlit by the sectors of the city that didn't fall with the destruction of the ancillary hub.

I expected to see dozens of police officers around the entrance to the central hub when I arrived. After all, I had just killed a half dozen soldiers in the lobby. Imagine my surprise when I didn't see one blue or red-light flashing, not even from an ambulance. The glass that had been obliterated by the SWAT team trying to take me down was completely restored, as were the pillars and pock-marked marble floor, which had been polished to a high shine. It was as if the battle never happened.

"No, no, no, no, no!" A holographic guard tried to intercept me as I marched towards the elevator. "You are not welcome here."

"Oh, don't be such a downer, Ferzalo," Rama's smooth

voice cooed as he stepped out from behind one of the pillars. "The way I see it, she provided a bit of entertainment—the likes of which I haven't seen in a long time."

"You!" I screamed, pulling my golden dagger and rushing him. "I'm really going to kill you!"

He snapped his fingers, and a force wave knocked me back; then another force held me in the air. "I appreciate your valor, but you cannot hope to take down the gods with a frontal assault. You have to be much sneakier than that."

I glowered at him. "And how many gods have you killed?"

"My fair share." He chuckled. "I think they even wrote a book about it once."

I struggled against my invisible binds, but they were tight and unforgiving. It took me back to my time in the Underworld, where the White Queen trapped me in black ichor. It was only Chelle that broke me free then, and now I had nobody on my side.

"Have you calmed down yet?" Rama asked. "I would like to let you go. I haven't quite finished here, and I do so hate a mess. However, I can't have you causing a fuss."

"I didn't cause a fuss. I was just trying to save myself. You caused a—"

"Me?" He placed his hand on his chest in mock surprise. "You have it all wrong. I didn't call those silly soldiers on you. That was a directive by the Board. They do not like what Nox did to you."

"You mean create a body for my soul, I assume?"

"Correct."

I furrowed my brow. "But it wasn't Nox. It was Hypnos."

He waved his hand dismissively. "You don't have to lie to protect her. Her fate is sealed. It's just the formality of her trial before they execute her, and your friend along with her."

"Friend?" I said, breathlessly. "You're talking about Chelle?"

"The dark-skinned gorgon with the snakes on her head, yes?" When I nodded, he bit his lip. "I'm afraid, then, that is who I mean."

I struggled harder. "No, I won't let that happen. Let me go. I have to save her."

He held up his hand. "You just might. With my help."

"Why would you want to help me?"

"Because the Board has been a blight on the universe for too long. They need to be taken care of, and we can't do that if our biggest benefactor has been killed."

"Nox?" I asked, but I already knew the answer.

"Yes," he said. "She has been working against them for a long time, trying to right the wrongs of the universe, always under the radar, until recently. She has taken quite a liking to you, it would seem."

"The feeling's not mutual," I said. "If you're working with her, then why did you turn me in?"

"I didn't. As for their pursuit, I did not stop them for two reasons," he said. "First, it would do neither of us any good if the Board found out what we were doing—"

"You keep saying the 'Board.' What does that mean?"

"They are a collection of the most powerful gods in the universe. Zeus, Brahma, Osiris, Tengri, Ukko, and Svarog."

"That's a lot of men." I'd heard about each of them in the Dream Realm in passing, but never as any collective entity.

"Yes, and they aim to keep it that way. Nox, and other forward thinkers like myself, don't much like that idea. We would like to see more equality on the Board, and so we fight against them in secret. Until now, that is, since Nox has made it nearly impossible to stay in the shadows."

"Considering she's a goddess of darkness, that is pretty ironic."

He laughed, a genuine laugh like I hadn't heard from him yet. "That is ironic, yes. Very good."

"Can you let me down, please?" I asked, pulling at my arms to free them.

"That depends. Are you going to help me? Help us?"

"I'm between a rock and a hard place, so I'm inclined to say yes. Besides, nobody kills Rose's girlfriend, or my friend."

"Very good." He snapped his fingers and I dropped to the ground. "I never told you the second reason for why I let them try to capture you."

I shook off the effects of the wave, rubbing my wrists as if they had been in shackles. "And what is that reason?"

"I needed to see if you were really as good as your reputation. It seems you are, which will be important in order to save her and your friend."

"Does this mean I don't have to find your stupid bow?"

Rama shook his head. "I will need it before the end, but for now, we have much bigger things to worry about. Namely, breaking into the most secure prison in the universe."

Of course it was another impossible thing to add to the list of already impossible things I'd done in my life. "Sounds like Tuesday."

CHAPTER 22

ARIEL

After the Fates diagnosed my problem, Queen Aine led me back into the castle. Without Chelle, the Fates were incapable of shattering the strong mental blocks that guarded my memories. Only the power of a god could give me back what was taken from me.

"But who would want to take my memories? And why?" It was a question that kept rattling through my brain as we passed the guards into the throne room.

"I can think of a couple of reasons," Queen Aine told me. "But none of them make complete sense. Instead of working in conjecture, it behooves us to call upon one of the only beings in Urgu who could have locked your memories away."

She meant Hypnos, of course. If I had met him before, then it was locked from me, like so much else from my past, apparently. Queen Aine fluttered to her throne and sat, then muttered a mantra that made the room glow a bright, emerald green. Even her body turned from its usual purple, and I had to squint to see anything through the brilliance of it all. After a few repetitions, the room flashed and then went dark, save for a white glow in its center.

"Why did you call me?" a voice rumbled. "I was in the middle of a card game, and I was winning."

"Sorry to disturb you, Hypnos." Queen Aine's voice had not an ounce of contrition to it. "But I thought you could explain something to my friend here."

Hypnos appeared, and I didn't feel the slight hint of recognition. He was a middle-aged man with salt and pepper hair, dressed in a white seersucker suit. His eyes were bright pink, like the magnificent dream orbs. If I had ever seen this man before, I would have known it.

"Who are you?" he asked, forehead crinkled.

"A-Ariel," I managed to say. Though I had spoken with Nox before, being in the presence of another god filled me with wonder.

He shook his head. "I don't know an Ariel."

"You might recall her better as the Drowned Princess," Queen Aine interjected. "You dusted a lot of people on her behalf."

He wagged his finger in the air, squinting. "Ah, yes, I remember now. Your mother was overthrown in a coup, and I saw her murderers brought to justice. Didn't you fall into the bottom of the sea, though?"

"Yes, I did, but Ursula, and your mother, saved me. They taught me how to live under the water, which is where I have been for three hundred years, until just this day."

"Fascinating," Hypnos said. "I have always found the sea boring, and the mermaids pedantic."

"They take some getting used to, but it's quite peaceful under the sea. There are no flying cars or highways."

"Making it even more tedious." Hypnos sighed and

turned to Queen Aine. "Is this really why you brought me back? To meet with a princess?"

"No. I brought you here to explain why her memories are locked, and to unlock them, since you're a god and all."

He threw his head back in disgust. "That's really my mother's thing, locking away memories."

"Well, she's gone, so it looks like you have to do a modicum of work to help us."

He stomped like a petulant child. "Fine. Let's get this over with." He grabbed my head, and everything went pink. All I could see was a luminous brightness, where Hypnos's voice echoed. "My, my. What a labyrinth you have weaved in here. My mother really did a number on you—well, this is interesting. There is another's fingerprints here, too. Girl, did you say you live with the mermaids?"

"Yes, I live with them now."

He took his hands off my head, and my eyes refocused to see the look of displeasure on his face. "I see. Well, this is very concerning then."

"What is?" I asked.

"The other fingerprints I saw on your memory were of the queen of the sea, Ursula."

I swallowed hard. "That's impossible. She has kept me safe for hundreds of years."

"I'm sorry to say this, girl, but I think she might be your captor. At the very least, she is as responsible for your lack of memory as my mother."

Ursula...my adopted mother...she helped do this to me? Why would she do such a thing?

"Can you remove the blocks?" Queen Aine asked, having returned to her glowing purple form. "It's very important."

Hypnos rubbed his forehead. "Not without potentially destroying her brain, which I assume you don't want."

Queen Aine glanced over at me. "No, I suppose we can't have that."

"Then your only choice is to go to the source," Hypnos said. "Return to the sea and speak with your mother. If anyone can unlock your memories—at least the ones she blocked off—it's her." He moved towards me. "But just know, whatever they hid from you, it has to be a very powerful secret. Are you sure you want to know it?"

I was never certain of much, but of this I was resolute. "Absolutely."

He placed his hand on my shoulder. "Then the gods' speed to you." He looked me in the eyes. "Yes, I see it now. You were once my champion, were you not? I chose you to take the throne from your mother."

"That's right."

He squeezed my shoulder, and a bright glow filled me. "Then take my blessing as it was once intended. It is not as much as it once was, but hopefully it will help you on your journey."

My eyes teared up in spite of me, like I had just acquired something I never knew I wanted. "Thank you."

"Don't thank me yet. Good things tend not to happen with people who get my blessing." He reached into his pocket and pulled out a pair of glasses. "Now, if you'll excuse me, I have a game to win."

"Don't you always win?" Queen Aine asked. "What's the fun in playing if you can't lose?"

"Why my dear, that's the only way I like to play."

CHAPTER 23

CHELLE

There was blessed silence for hours after Nox's confession. I had nothing to say to her, and I wasn't in a forgiving mood. A few times she looked over at me and I met her gaze with an unsympathetic glare so that she'd turn back to her dingy cell. The silence, while welcome, was not absolute. Moans and whimpers came from the cells around me, and the ship had its own mechanical groans.

I spent my time trying unsuccessfully to find a way to break the seal of the cell walls and escape. It was a fool's errand, as I didn't even know where in the ever-loving blazes we were, or how to make it back to Earth if somehow I found a way out of the cell, but it was better than succumbing to whatever fate Athena and the other gods had in store for me.

Despite the creaking of the ship, the cells themselves were constructed by a master, apparently forged from a single piece of metal, smooth and flawless. Perhaps I could have burned through it, but my magic didn't work within the confines of its walls. Runes were carved onto the edges, and while I couldn't decipher them, I understood their meaning easy enough. They were meant to quell all magic, rendering us powerless.

Though fruitless, searching for a way out passed the time until, with a final lurch, the ship came to a stop. I toppled over and crashed into the far side of my cell. Judging by the sounds from the other cells, I wasn't the only one knocked sideways.

"Listen to me," Nox said, crawling towards me. "I know you hate me, and that's fine, but you must stay close once we reach the Crystal Keep."

"I want nothing to do with you," I growled, standing up.

"If you hope to stay alive in this place, then you'll do as I say. I can only protect you if we are close together."

"I have seen what your protection brings, and I will pass."

The prison door slid open, and Nox scampered back to the edge of her cell. Athena stomped in, her black suit replaced with a red cloak, her blonde hair pulled back into a slick ponytail.

"Listen up, maggots. We have reached the Crystal Keep where you'll be held until your trial, should you be lucky enough to have one. These cells will open, and you will line up in two single-file lines. If you break rank, we will shoot you dead on the spot."

She cleared her throat. "For those of you who wish to stay alive a while longer, step through the doors and down the ramp for processing. May the other gods have mercy on your souls, for I have none."

With that, she snapped her fingers and the doors to the cells swung open. Before I could step outside, a wild-eyed werewolf rushed from their cell and leapt at Athena. The goddess didn't even bat an eye. Lasers erupted on either side of her, frying the werewolf to a crisp.

"Any other heroes?" She smirked, turning first to Nox and then to me and then the others, but there were no heroics in any of us. "Good. Then form up."

I inched out of my cell and met Nox in the center walkway. Avoiding her eyes, I turned back to the other prisoners. Eight of them lined the cell block, and, aside from a couple of demons, were completely foreign to me. One had orange skin and three eyes, with suckers protruding from both sides of its head. Next to them slumped a slug-like green grub with slimy skin that glistened in the overhead light. Behind those two and a pair of gray demons stood a purple being that looked like two bodies fused together through a mesh of arms and legs. Finally, behind them all was a large creature with various limbs protruding from it and no head that I could see upon a quick glance.

Athena didn't bother handcuffing us as she turned and led us down the corridor.

"Do you really have a plan?" I whispered to Nox.

"This isn't really the time," she hissed back. "Which is why I told you to stay close."

Athena turned back to us, and I shut my mouth. Halfway down the next cabin, a ramp had been lowered to the ground, and an ominous orange glow seeped into the room. I stepped down the gangplank onto the foreboding world underneath me.

"Follow the crystal golems inside." She pointed to a squad of humanoid figures shimmering the same glow as the massive crystal fortress. "As you can see, there is no escape. So, abandon all hope, for you have been forsaken."

I had heard that before, about abandoning hope, but I

would not do so. Even in the darkest times—especially in the darkest times—the most punk rock thing you can do in a world trying to steal every ounce of goodness from you was hope.

If all else failed, there was one thing I knew for sure. Rose would come for me, even if she had to travel across the universe to do it.

CHAPTER 24
RED

The Obsidian Spindle on Servasi 9 was built on the side of a craggily hill alongside a stone church that represented the most revered and ancient locale on the whole planet, along with the most ignored. The inhabitants of that world had a penchant for blowing up everything about their civilization every few decades when something better and more exciting came along. The planet was in a constant state of renewal, with new construction beginning on their buildings nearly as soon as they were finished, in a vicious, never-ending cycle.

I hated cultures that devalued the old to worship on the altar of the new. Even California was too modern for my tastes. I preferred traveling to places that appreciated their history; with apartments from the 1500s retrofitted with indoor plumbing and pubs older than the Norman invasion. I felt safe in those places, like I could get my footing under me and know that things wouldn't change.

"It's an eyesore, isn't it?" Rama said with a grunt, gesturing at the ancient buildings. We were headed up the hill towards the Obsidian Spindle.

"I love the older style," I replied. "It's the only part of your planet I like."

He rolled his eyes. "You would like it. Tradition is a crutch used to keep people submissive. The more we can live in the present and abandon our past, the freer we become." He glanced at me. "I wouldn't expect a human to understand that, though."

"What I don't understand is you," I replied. "You seem to despise me, and yet you asked me to help you."

"You can hate a hammer and still understand its usefulness as a blunt object. You are my blunt object, the one I have begrudgingly agreed to use because all of my more elegant tools are ineffective against the problem we face."

"That is one way to gain my loyalty, I guess," I replied. "I mean, what girl doesn't want to be compared to tools?"

"I wasn't trying to woo you, Gabrielle." He chuckled. "Does that disappoint you?"

I snorted derisively. "Absolutely not. The last thing I would ever do is fall in love with a god. You are self-centered egomaniacs, only happy when people fall to their knees and worship you."

"Worship is an odd word, but I cannot deny I enjoy it when people fall on their knees before me."

"That's disgusting, but not surprising, given the source."

"I do not need your approval," he said. "But I do require your loyalty, and your trust, for this to work."

"Those are things you must earn, and since you just tried to get me arrested, I would say you're pretty far off from gaining either of those things from me."

We arrived on the flat area where the Obsidian Spindle stood. Rama brushed his fingertips along its face until he found a groove where he could insert the key he had on a cord around his neck.

"Under normal circumstances, we could spend time building trust between each other, but Nox and Chelle have been arrested and their trial will start soon. If we cannot save them quickly, then all of our plans will be for naught."

"I believe you want Nox freed, and that you understand Chelle's rescue is a condition of my help, and I further believe that you will not betray me until your aims are met, but once they are, I expect to find a knife in my back sooner than later."

"My love." He smiled as the white door slid open in the base of the Spindle. "I would never stab you in the back when stabbing you in the front is so much more fun." He held out his hand. "However, if you can at least believe that I want those things and would never betray you until those goals are met, then let that be the basis of our trust, and we will work from there."

I placed my hand in his. "An uneasy alliance is better than none, I suppose. Still, I will not be walking behind you just yet. You go first."

"I'm not looking for somebody to follow behind me, Gabrielle, but stand beside me, as my equal."

CHAPTER 25

ROSE

After finishing at his house, Lenny followed us back to my apartment, where he proceeded to stare at my kitchen table from across the living room for over an hour, clicking his teeth and sucking his gums as he tilted his head from one side to the other. Every time I thought he had something to say, he would open his mouth, and then close it again in a pout of silent frustration.

Meanwhile, I went about straightening my house from the invasion of the FBI agents who had taken over. They hadn't bothered to wipe their feet, or clean the cups they took from my cupboard, so I had enough nervous cleaning to do while Jamil sat at the kitchen table making idle chit-chat about people I either never met or didn't like much.

"What about the nice girl with the earrings who lived in the parking lot with us?" I snapped my fingers. "What was her name? She had dreadlocks."

"Greta?" Jamil asked. "She graduated and moved to Fresno to work as a social worker, just like she always dreamed about."

"That's nice," I said. "It seems like everybody moved on. And what about you? Did you ever leave the parking lot?"

"I tried, but it's expensive out there, so I went back earlier this year. It's completely different now. Back when we lived there, there was a big ole bit of community support. People respected each other, but now...now if you ask somebody to turn off their lights so you can sleep, they just look at you funny and flip you the bird."

"That sucks." I bit my lip. "I really loved that parking lot."

"Bull," Jamil said. "There is nothing to love about living in your car."

"We had a van," I said. "Chelle and I, and it was enough for us. It was the last time I think we were truly free. You know I've barely seen Chelle for the past two years, and now she's gone again. What I wouldn't give to get back to those halcyon days of that parking lot, when the biggest trouble on my mind was whether I'd get fired."

"And whether you would be able to buy insulin," Jamil added. "At least you aren't days from death anymore."

It was true. All of this had started with a diabetic coma because I couldn't afford my insulin. That wasn't an issue anymore, as between Hypnos's endowment and the FBI's healthcare, I was no longer in desperate need of finding a spare thousand dollars every month just to keep myself alive.

"I guess the grass is always greener." I sighed. "I really was happy these last couple of months, though. Even if I didn't see Chelle a lot, at least I fell asleep in her arms every night."

"Gross," Jamil said. "Also, cute."

"Would you two quit chattering over there?" Lenny snapped. "I'm trying to concentrate."

Jamil swerved her head to him. "You've been staring into the middle distance for an hour, and it's boring as hell. Excuse us for trying to entertain ourselves."

"Technically, Hell isn't that boring," I said, instantly regretting being *that* person. "Sorry."

"I'm not staring into the abyss, you nincompoop." Lenny pushed his hands outward and a shimmer of blue shot into the air. "I'm waiting for the universe to speak to me."

"What is that?" I said, squinting at the blue light. Cheyenne joined me, weaving through my legs and growling at the light.

"It's exactly what I feared." He sat back on the couch. "Your fiancée has been taken by the God Squad."

Jamil tried to keep a straight face, but she couldn't help chuckling. "I'm sorry, the God Squad? That is the least terrifying name for a thing ever."

"It's just a nickname. They're the Celestial Enforcement Department of the United Federation of Gods. They work for the Board administering their rules on the universe, and it seems like your paramour has gotten on their bad side."

"Wait," I said. "So, she was kidnapped by the gods?"

"Not kidnapped, arrested." He sniffed the air. "This smells like Athena to me. You said Chelle was reincarnated from the Dream Realm?"

"That's right," I said.

"Yeah, the gods hate that kind of thing. It's against all sorts of their laws. The good news is that they are so overburdened it often takes centuries for them to pull the trigger on an arrest, but this must have been a special case, especially if they got Athena involved."

"Okay, I'm only understanding about a third of what

you are saying, so can you please speak plainly to me, like I am a child?"

He leaned forward, resting his elbows on his knees. "Your fiancée has been arrested and taken to the Celestial Realm for trial. She'll be held there until the kangaroo court that is the Crystal Keep rules on her fate, which will likely mean execution. I'm sorry."

I shook my head. "I'm not going to let that happen. How do I get to the Celestial Realm?"

"The only way is to be taken by a god."

I held out my hand. "Then let's go."

"Not me. I'm not pure enough to gain access. They are very strict about that kind of thing. You need somebody who is 100 percent god to get through the gates. I hope you have powerful friends, missy."

"Luckily, I do."

There was a knock on the door and Cheyenne rushed over, barking like a maniac. I approached slowly and pushed open the door, ready for a fight. It was Agent Edwards.

"It's good to see you're alive." He held up a cage with a rat in it. "And not this rat that you had us chasing for much of the day."

"I'm alive," I said. "Sorry for leaving, but you weren't being helpful, and I didn't have the energy to deal with you telling me I couldn't go search for Chelle."

"Your girlfriend has been abducted and your first thought is to ditch the people here to protect you? That's not very smart."

"Fiancée. And you're probably right, but now that you're here, I need your help."

"Of course. After all you've put us through today, there's nothing the FBI wants more than to help you."

I ignored his sarcasm. "That's good to hear. So how did you find that rat?"

"We have a scanner that pings the location of any tracker we implanted."

I pouted, trying to look as pathetic as possible. "Do you think we could borrow one?"

He groaned. "I don't want to know, do I?"

"Not unless you want to start a war between the gods and Earth," Lenny called from the couch.

"Yup," Agent Edwards said. "I definitely don't want to know." He reached into his pocket and pulled out a box roughly the size of my cell phone. "All of your trackers are programmed into it. All you have to do is turn it on and choose which one you want to ping."

I took the box. "Thank you, Agent Edwards."

"Don't thank me," he replied. "Because I never saw you today, right?"

Jamil, Lenny, and I looked at each other. "Saw who?"

"Perfect." He smiled. "I don't suppose I'll be seeing you again."

"You might yet," I said. "I have no intention of dying out there."

"Nobody does," he replied, and then he walked away, leaving me to my fate. "And yet, they do just the same."

CHAPTER 26
NIMUE

Every board in Baba's cabin creaked, and the gaps between them revealed glowing eyes in the darkness below. Cassandra and I followed the sound of swishing to a small wooden Spindle, where a hunched woman with small hands worked to spin black wool into thread.

As we neared, the Spindle stopped, and the woman looked up at us. I expected horrific eyes and an ancient jaw, but she looked kind—sweet, even, with warm eyes and a gentle smile. She beckoned us closer.

"Do not be fooled by her gentle demeanor," Cassandra whispered. "She will rip out your heart as quickly as look at you."

"Why must you paint me in such a way, Cassandra?" Baba's voice was lyrical and charming, nothing like I expected. "I am as kind as your heart. If you treat me with respect, I will do the same to you."

"Of course," Cassandra said, dipping her head to the ground. "I don't mean to offend you, great Baba."

"Stop your groveling, Cassandra. It's unbecoming." Baba studied me up and down. "The years have been kind to you, my love. What I wouldn't give to wear your skin as my own."

She placed her cold hand on my cheek. I fought my instinct to back away and instead let her caress the side of my face, down to my neck. Her hands were warm after working them on the spindle.

"Enough, Baba," Cassandra said. "We had a deal, and you agreed to it."

Baba smiled. "I had no idea what kind of skin I was dealing with. It's almost a pity to destroy it."

"Destroy it?" I asked. "I don't like the sound of that."

Baba snapped her head towards Cassandra. "You didn't tell her. How lovely. Leaving me to do the dirty work."

"I know that something must be done to make me fit in with monsters. Otherwise, the king will destroy me himself, and for his pleasure. I just didn't think it would mean destroying my skin, which I've quite grown to like."

"But it is not yours, is it, Nimue? You stole it from that little Bernadette girl with the help of a demon, just like I stole from so many who wronged me."

I bit the inside of my cheek. "You do not scare me, great Baba. I have known your kind on my world, and I have seen things you would not believe. I survived the Nightmare Realm. I can survive here."

Baba chuckled. "You may believe so, but the Nightmare Realm is child's play in comparison to the Dark Planet. Epiales is a joke."

"On that we can agree," I replied. "Now, what must you do to my skin?"

Baba looked at Cassandra and back to me, then paused. "The king has four concubines, princesses that he has turned into his personal guard. They are his prized possessions, the daughters of former rulers whom he twisted to his wicked ways."

"My sisters," Cassandra said.

"You were a princess?" I asked, raising my eyebrows. "And now you live in a shack."

"It is preferable to the alternative, living in the castle, subjected to his violent...delights."

"So, you aim to take my skin?" I asked, turning back to Baba. I didn't want to ask what she meant by violent delights. "Like with Cassandra."

"That was not her original punishment," Baba said, standing with a groan. Her bones creaked like the joints in a door. After her knees snapped into place, she made a circle around me. "She was once considerably more ethereal. Each princess was given a different form, and I believe I can do the same to you." She met my face again and smiled. "Don't worry. Your precious Rapunzel will be able to fix you up again, should you succeed."

"And if I don't?"

"Then you should hope the king keeps you in his harem, because it would be nothing compared to the torture I would inflict on you."

"Got it." I swallowed, hard. "Kill the king or be tortured for eternity."

"Once I begin," Baba said. "Our deal is bound in blood. Only the crown of the king will finalize our arrangement. Do you consent?"

I looked over at Cassandra, who offered no response. "I thought you already agreed."

"I made the deal," Cassandra replied. "But as the one who will kill the King in Yellow, you must be the one to agree to it."

"I don't like this, but yes, I consent."

"Then let us begin." Baba raised a long finger. "Take a deep breath."

I did as she commanded, and she touched my chest. When she did, it felt as if the universe reached into my chest and pulled it open. My skin gurgled and ripped, splintering from the middle of my chest outward, leaving a chasm in the center of it, filled with thousands of stars.

The splinters didn't stop there, though. They continued up my neck and down my arms, until the bottom of my jaw was completely subsumed by a darkness which then crawled up my cheeks and into my eyes. My hair turned to a dark, blood red, matching the edges of the splinters. I breathed in and felt the air leave through the caverns of my body.

When she was done, Baba led me to a mirror. I expected to cower in fear and despise my new body, but looking into the mirror, eyeing the red of my skin and the expanse in my chest, I had never felt more beautiful in all my life; I had become an entire galaxy contained inside a person, my own little universe spinning, with me in the center.

"What do you think, deary?" she asked quietly.

"I always knew I was the center of the galaxy," I said, running my hands around the cracks in my chest. "And now you have simply proved it."

"Your confidence will serve you well in the capital. Or it will get you killed."

I looked over my shoulder through the mirror, catching Baba's eyes. "The king will die, and you will have your crown. Count on it."

"Many have tried, deary," the old woman replied, placing her bony fingers on my collarbone, inches from them being lost inside the cavern in my chest. "I'll reserve judgement until I see it with my own eyes."

CHAPTER 27

ARIEL

Cefus sent a carriage, but he didn't come along to escort me home, so I was alone with my thoughts the entire way back to my mother's castle. Descending into the underwater sanctuary of the sea was supposed to be a joyous occasion, but after learning that my adopted mother had locked my memories away, it felt like I had returned to a jail cell from which I would never leave again, left alone with a gnawing pain deep in my heart.

I had so many questions, but I feared the answers. What if she truly was the one who locked my memories away? What if I was brought to the mermaids for a reason, and they feigned affection for me while having nothing but malice in their hearts? And what if Ursula lied to me and told me she had nothing to do with it? Which fate would be worse?

For so long, I'd taken comfort in the darkness of the sea and feared even a glimmer of light, but what if that darkness I so loved was nothing but a convenient lie spun to keep me docile, and the light was there to burn those shadows away and let me see the truth?

The last of the light from the surface faded and I found myself engulfed by the darkness once again; my throat tightened, and my hands shook. I trusted Ursula with my very life, and the thought of confronting her, of demanding the truth, sent shivers up my spine. The carriage opened when it reached the castle.

"Welcome home, princess," Cefus said, helping me down. I had long ago taken off the shoes bestowed to me by the Emerald City and left them in the carriage. The dress tangled with my legs and constricted my movements as I tried to swim, but I still wore it. When we reached the coral doors of my mother's throne room, I did something I hadn't in a long time and placed my feet on the ground. Though the urchins and coral were made to look like carpet, they were equal parts hard and squishy under my feet, but I did not dare rise again into the water. I came back as an emissary for the surface, and as such I decided to walk on the ground like I had done on the surface.

"Ah, my sweet princess," Ursula said as I entered the throne room. "You have returned, and you look beautiful. The surface agrees with you."

"Thank you, Mother." I swallowed, tasting the sea water. "I did my best to do you proud."

"I have always been proud of you, my sweet thing. Now, what did they want from the surface?"

I knew it would be one of her first questions, and yet I had hoped against hope that we could have some more moments of pleasantness before we dove into the cold, hard truths that I needed to drop on her.

"They wanted to know where I hid the left eye of Rapunzel." I said the words steadily, and without emotion. My eyes never wavered from Ursula.

"And—and what did you tell them?" Ursula stammered, something she never did. Normally, she was as steady as the coral and as strong as the great blue whale.

"I told them the truth, that I had no idea what they were talking about."

"Oh," Ursula composed herself, but her eyes still darted all around the room. "Of course."

"They seemed to think that I knew where it was, though. They were so adamant about it that they took me to the Fates, and Hypnos...who told me that somebody locked my memories away."

She blinked. "That's—preposterous. I've never heard anything so ludicrous."

I summoned all the courage in my body and took a step forward. "What did you do to me, Mother?"

Her face moved from cautious to angry in an instant. "How dare you—after all I've given you, to accuse me of something so heinous!"

"Answer the question, Mother. Who locked my memories away?"

"I have no idea," she blustered, lifting her chin. "When you came to me, you were exactly as you are now."

"The entirety of the Dream Realm is in trouble, Mother. If we don't get the left eye of Rapunzel, there will be a reckoning. Everyone, including the mermaids, will be in danger."

"Piffle." Ursula waved dismissively. "That is what they said during the Battle of the Emerald City."

I trembled now, feeling anger. "If we had intervened then, many lives might have been spared."

She leaned forward and hissed, "And by staying neutral we saved all our people."

"My people live on the surface. I have been kept from them, and I thought that was because I truly loved it down here. But now I wonder.... So, please, if you have any feelings towards me, tell me the truth. What did you do to me?"

Ursula's face shifted from fury to boredom. She gave a tight smile, and then tipped her head. "Very well, Ariel. I will tell you the truth. If that's what you want."

"It's all I ever wanted," I said. "For people to be honest with me."

"Nox brought you to us, scared and alone, saying that you had knowledge buried in your head that needed to stay buried until the appropriate time. She asked if I would take you in, and I agreed. When you arrived, she had already locked a part of your mind from me."

I digested this information. "Nox did this to me?"

"That's correct," she said. "I'm so sorry to tell you this." She descended the stairs and wrapped her arms around me. "I never wanted anything but the best for you."

There was something in her words that rang hollow. "So, you never altered my mind, Mother?"

"Of course not," she replied, arm still holding me.

"Because it seems like anytime I've tried to explore the area beyond the coral, something stops me. I can't help but wonder...why? How?" I pulled away from her. "And then I realized that it's very possible I keep finding something out there, and you keep locking those memories away from me."

"That's—" Ursula looked me into the eye, her hands on my shoulders. "Fine, no more lying. That's exactly what happened, and I regret nothing. My job as your mother is to keep you safe, and that is what I have done."

I shook her off of me. "You lied to me!"

"Every parent lies to their children. It's part of growing up! Now you know the truth."

I closed my eyes to calm down and spoke slowly. "Give

me my memories back. They are mine, and I deserve to know the truth."

"What is to stop me from wiping this incident from your memory, too?"

"I believe you love me, I do, and that you want the best for me. I have to trust you not to do anything against my wishes again."

She sighed and held out her hands. "I can't give them all back, but I can give you the ones I kept from you. Only Nox can unlock the rest."

"Give me back what you can," I whispered. "And let me make my own choice about what to do with it."

"Fine," Ursula said. She touched my forehead, and suddenly, everything went white.

CHAPTER 28

CHELLE

It took a moment for my eyes to adjust to the brightness of the Crystal Keep. A million stars shone down, and though the sky was dark, the Keep's brilliance forced me to squint.

"Do not stop until you reach the inner sanctum!" Athena shouted. Four crystal golems flanked us while she marched us to a glittering door, which slid open at her approach.

The Crystal Keep was not nearly as grand inside. The walls and floor shimmered a hundred different colors, but the light barely reflected from them. Still, there was just enough light bouncing from every direction to nullify any shadows and make Nox, the god of darkness, uneasy.

Two burly soldiers in full riot gear held clipboards and checked us off one by one. Once they were assured that we were all presented and accounted for, save for the charred werewolf lying on the floor of the ship, the soldiers made their way to the front of the room.

"Strip!" Athena screamed at us.

"Why?" My response earned me a swift backhand.

"You are covered with filth from your horrid planet, and

from your trek across the galaxy. But more importantly, you strip because I said so. Do you understand?"

I wanted so badly to fight, but that would have been a stupid move. I had no power here, and nobody to back me up. I needed to bide my time. Rose would come for me, somehow. Instead of causing a bigger scene by attacking my captor, I wiped the blood from my mouth and pulled off my clothes.

The golems collected all of our things and then brought us into another room, where they hosed us down with a milky substance, and then threw shimmering glitter onto our bodies that burned my nose. When they were finished, my eyes were blurry, and I could barely see the guard who shoved a silver jumpsuit into my hands. I pulled it on, without getting a chance to dry off, and it stuck uncomfortably to my body.

A guard snapped on a new pair of glowing blue restraints on my arms, legs, and neck. "This will give you free range of motion," the guard said. "But also it restrains you. Act up and 10,000 volts will shoot through you in an instant, immobilizing you."

"I get it." My voice was scratchy and hoarse from inhaling the glitter. "You own us now."

"Exactly."

They led us all into a cell block filled with cells rising up into the ceiling a hundred feet above.

"This is where I leave you!" Athena shouted. "Nox! Chelle! You're with me. The rest of you, get comfortable in your new home." She dragged me forward with one arm while she pulled at Nox with the other.

"What are you doing?" I said, struggling against her grip. "Where are you taking me?"

"The Board wants to start your trial immediately.

You've caused a lot of fuss," Athena said. "Personally, I think the reports about the two of your exploits have been exaggerated. After all, you barely put up a fight when I came for you. Waste of my time if you ask me, but my job is not to question why. It is merely do or die." She shoved me. "Now move. I have plans tonight and they don't involve you."

CHAPTER 29

RED

I had been through a portal in the Obsidian Spindle a dozen times in the past several months, so the tingling sensation was a surprise. My heart jolted in my chest, and when Rama squeezed my hand, I realized I hadn't taken a breath in several seconds. His touch sent a shockwave through me, and my eyes focused to realize we were no longer in the portal.

"Are you okay?" he said, cradling my head. "The Celestial Realm is sometimes hard for mortals to adjust to, but I thought with your special pedigree you would be okay. I should have prepared you better."

I nodded as I pushed myself to stand with Rama's aid. "I'm fine, I think."

My collapse had gathered a crowd, who watched as I struggled to my feet and used the wall to steady myself. It wasn't until I had a moment to catch my bearings that I realized that the crowd wasn't there for me but had been queueing to use a collection of portals in the long marble room where we stood.

"Where are we?" I asked, watching the gods stumble

forward slowly before they disappeared into the half dozen white portals.

"This is the junction for every Obsidian Spindle in the known universe. From the Celestial Realm, you can get anywhere in the entire cosmos in an instant."

"That's convenient." I lurched past him into the street, where I sucked in the cool, crisp air. When my stomach stopped tumbling, I stood up straight and looked into the sky, where a million stars twinkled back at me.

"It's always night here," he said. "There is not one star this realm rotates around. Instead, they all rotate around us."

I couldn't help but laugh, even though it burned my chest to do so. "Now it makes sense how you gods can be so arrogant. The whole of the cosmos rotates around you."

He pressed his hands into my shoulders. "It's really unwise to insult us so blatantly out in the open. We never know who is watching."

"Right," I replied. "Don't want to infuriate any gods. Well, lead the way then, since you know where you're going."

Rama offered me his arm to lean against, and I ashamedly took it from him. I wasn't used to being some damsel to be rescued, but this realm unsettled my stomach and stiffened my legs. Rama assured me that I would adjust, but the air was like a toxic poison coursing through me, and instead of getting better, every step weakened me.

As I followed Rama through the city, I noticed the anachronistic nature of the buildings. A sleek crystal high-rise stood next to a 14th century brownstone, and both stood caddy corner to an 18th century brick building. The gods that passed through the streets also spanned the ages, one dressed in a tunic, the next wearing a zoot suit and parasol, followed by a man in torn pants and a pointed mohawk.

"You gods sure have an odd way about you," I whispered to Rama on our way down a cobblestone street.

"We have our eccentricities. When you have lived for as long as us in such varied planets, we pick and choose the fashion we like best from them all, and often our dress doesn't make sense to any but us."

I passed by a woman wearing a pink hoop skirt, a nose ring, and pompadour with her arms fully tattooed with flowers and pandas. She was walking with a man in a long beard twisted with beeswax, wearing a tunic with a pair of cheap sunglasses.

"I suppose it's nice that you have that kind of freedom."

"It's one of the few freedoms we are afforded, and I often think that we are given these small graces to mask the fact that we are all pawns in the Board's machinations."

"I thought you were all free to do anything you chose."

"That is what we would like you to think, but it is not the truth."

He turned us up a side street, darker than the others we'd been using, that reeked of rotten food. Apparently, even in the Celestial Realm, back alleys still smelled like garbage. We stopped at a red door with a bronze gorgon head chomping a brass knocker in its mouth. When Rama walked up, the gorgon sprang to life and groaned.

"You again? Here to stir up trouble?"

"My dear," Rama cooed, "I never stir up trouble. I simply point out the trouble that existed without me."

"Save the charm for somebody with a libido," the gorgon replied with an eye roll. "Password."

"Bravada." He smiled. "Something I have in spades."

She shook her head. "Not anymore. New month, new password. I sent it to your email account three days ago."

Rama grumbled and pulled out a phone, swiping through its contents.

I blinked. "Gods have email?"

"Of course. Do you think we would allow something like that for humanity without having it for ourselves? We are stuck in our ways, but we are not stupid." He continued scrolling. "Junk. Junk. Junk. Ah, here we go—" He stopped. "Really? Is this a dig at me?"

"Maybe it is, maybe it's not," the gorgon replied. "Password."

Rama sighed and mumbled, "I'm sorry."

The gorgon laughed so hard that the brass ring almost came out of its mouth. "Two words I never thought I would hear you say."

"I'm glad I could amuse you," Rama said. "Now, please open the door, Patrisiol. Our friend needs to sit down."

"Another conquest?" Patrisiol said. "You have finally run out of gods who fall for your schtick that you've moved to pathetic humans. I didn't think you would ever stoop so low."

"Hey!" I shouted at her, taking a step forward and promptly falling to the ground.

Rama pulled me up again. "Now you've upset my friend, so I will ask you again. Let us in."

"Very well. I forgot you can't take a joke," Patrisiol said. The door creaked open.

"I'm sorry about her," Rama said, guiding me through the door by the small of my back. "She's a pain, but you won't find a more loyal guard in all the realms of man or god."

"I just need a seat," I replied. "And maybe a drink to calm my humors."

"Then you've come to the right place," Rama replied. The hallway broke open into an old-fashioned speakeasy. "We have the best drinks in the universe."

CHAPTER 30

ROSE

I popped two Ambien and faded off to sleep. Over the past couple of months, I had started taking them like candy. I wasn't proud of it, but they were the only thing that allowed me to sleep deeply enough to get me into the Dream Realm. If I didn't visit it every night, I woke up cranky and annoyed the next day.

Ever since Chelle returned to me, I had avoided the Land of Oz, finding solace in the Mistreach, where Anansi once ruled, or in the Mountains near Agrona's keep, which had been buried in an avalanche after the end of our war with the Nightmare Realm. I didn't want to be dragged into any drama, and the Emerald City was full of it, but there was no way to avoid it anymore. I needed a god to bring me to the Celestial Realm, and the only ones I knew lived in the Emerald City. Unless, of course, I wanted to kill myself and speak with Persephone, but falling asleep was easier. Persephone was a distant Plan B.

I had mastered Hypnos's blessing and used it to enter the Dream Realm at the entrance to Queen Aine's castle. Many people gazed in wonder at the emerald gems that

Nox and Hypnos used to construct the new castle, but I found the whole thing gaudy and the carved stone inside of it a sad replacement for all the artwork that once adorned its halls.

The guards bent the knee quickly upon my arrival and allowed me to enter quickly and without any fuss. I was, after all, the only living former queen of Urgu. My feet echoed across the gem floors as I followed the sinewy paths to the throne room. The route was long and circuitous to prevent any who invaded from making their way easily to the queen.

Lady Lynx stood at the black door, waiting for me. "Welcome Queen Rose. I heard you had come to call on us and could not be happier that you have graced us with your presence."

"I appreciate your formality, as always, Lady Lynx. However, I am in quite a rush. I need to see Nox or, barring that, Hypnos. Can you point me to them?"

Lady Lynx crinkled her nose. "Nox is gone. We have not seen her in some months, and Hypnos, as he always seems to be, is caught up in games of chance and indisposed."

"Where is he?"

"Are you sure you would not like to entreat with Queen Aine? I'm sure she would be quite pleased to see you."

"Unless she can get me into the Celestial Realm, it will just be a waste of time. Now, please, can you show me to Hypnos."

"But—"

I held up my hand. "I am trying to be polite, Lady Lynx. Please do not confuse my question as an invitation to equivocate. What I meant was 'show me to Hypnos now.' Understand?"

Lady Lynx sighed, and I felt for her. Her job was to

protect the castle and the rulers who lived there. It must have been hard to eat so much crow when people demanded things of you that were outside of your control. That being said, I would not hesitate to steamroll her again, given the need.

She led me through more corridors until we exited the castle into a sculpture garden. "Have you seen your likeness yet?"

I shook my head. "No, I missed the dedication."

"If you would indulge me."

I winced as I smiled. "All right, but I don't have a lot of time."

"I'll be quick as a bunny."

She walked straight through the grassy knoll. Sculptures of marble and obsidian rose from the ground, depicting the great rulers and deeds of the past. Queen Aine's bust flew proudly over the Emerald City in one, and in another Hypnos's eyes shimmered as he held out his arms for all Dreamers.

Lady Lynx stopped and gestured up. It was a striking likeness, towering over the other statues. Fire rose from my hand and light shone from my eyes. Under my foot, a bronze plinth was inscribed with "Queen Rose. The Dreamer. Hero of our age."

"Do you like it?" Lady Lynx asked, studying me.

I smiled. "I often forget what I did for this place. It feels like an entirely different person saved you all."

"They sing songs about you, Queen Rose. Sects have grown to worship you as a god."

"That can't be true."

"It is, truly. They even discussed making you one of the Six when they rebuilt the temple."

"Well, that's silly."

"Not to these people," Lady Lynx said. "You are a legend to them, and without you, none of this would exist."

I blushed in spite of myself. "Well, let's not get a big head about it. I have more business to attend."

"No rest for the wicked," Lady Lynx said, before correcting herself. "Or the virtuous, as the case may be."

"I can't be sure they aren't the same thing," I said. "What is virtuous to one person is wicked to another."

She nodded. "Well said, my lady. Speaking of, let me show you to our feckless man-child god."

"Oh, I'm sure he's not as bad as all that," I said. We weaved our way through the statues.

"You're right," Lady Lynx replied with a raised eyebrow. "He's much worse."

CHAPTER 31
NIMUE

I couldn't stop looking down at my alabaster skin, cracked with red veins and black abyss with the stars of the universe spiraling through it. Cassandra took quick glimpses at me as we walked out of the forest, but she mostly kept her eyes forward until we reached town.

At the edge of the one-lane road that cut through town was a black carriage wrapped in leather, four gaunt horses yoked to its front. Atop the carriage a black-eyed man with a hollow smile tipped his top hat to us.

"Ma'am," he said. He didn't give me a second glance. "I have been chartered to bring you to Carcosa."

Cassandra curtseyed. "Desecrated greetings."

"And to you," the pasty man returned. "May your trip be filled with horrors unimaginable."

"And unspeakable." Cassandra pulled herself into the cart.

I joined her in the cab. "Unspeakable and unimaginable horrors? Don't you think that is a little much?"

"You have not been here long, and yet you judge us so harshly?" She sighed. "Perhaps if you keep an open mind, you will learn something about the universe. Not everybody believes in the honor of beauty."

I cocked my head. "I have seen things in the Nightmare Realm that would turn your stomach and conversed with the darkness immortal, allowing it to fill me."

"And you fought it," she said. "You fought the darkness, did you not? I can feel it in every pore of your skin. You looked upon the darkness, and it filled you with dread."

"No...well, maybe at first, but then I learned to love it, to cherish that part of myself."

"And why do you not wield the power of darkness now?"

"Because the Face—Rapunzel has given me a new gift."

Cassandra shook her head. "No, you lost the darkness's trust before you ever met her. Tell me, did you try to control it? Did you treat it as a slave, and not a friend?"

"How—how did you know that?"

Her lips curled upwards. It wasn't quite a smile, but it was the closest she could manage. "You seem like the type."

The carriage lurched forward, and I had to steady myself against the doors. "Don't begin to think you know me."

"I know enough. I know you find beauty to be good, and ugliness to be evil. I know you believe that I am hideous, because I do not fit your definition of beauty."

"I—"

"Don't!" A fire grew in her eyes. "Do not lie to me. I am not one of your sycophants. I know I do not conform to your standard of beauty, but there is beauty in me, even in what you find revolting. Just because something looks like a monster doesn't mean it is so."

"I know that."

"No, you don't. Down in your bones you want to put

things in a bucket, good and bad, beautiful and ugly, worth saving and worth casting aside. Just like the gods who left us all to die in this place."

She didn't know anything about me, and yet she was all too comfortable putting me in her own bucket, and judging me...underestimating me, just like everyone else. No matter what I did, it was never enough for people. I was on a carriage, ready to kill a king for these people, and Cassandra still only saw a monster who wasn't good enough to treat with respect.

But I didn't need her respect. I only needed Rapunzel's magic, and I would do anything to attain it. Even the small taste she'd blessed me with filled me with an energy I forgot I missed, and if I could have more, I would eat whatever crow I had to, even if it meant swallowing Cassandra's trite observations.

"You should try to get some sleep," she said, resting her head on the wall of the carriage. "It will all happen very fast once we get to the capital."

"And what will happen?" I asked.

"At the turn of every season, the king fetes his loyal followers with a feast that lasts for three days. Once a year, he holds the grandest feast of them all, the Hellonic Ball. As a princess to this kingdom, though fallen from his grace, I am granted an audience with him, and as my guest, so are you. He will greet us, as is his duty, and you will use that opportunity to kill him."

"He must be guarded by a hundred soldiers."

"They will be nearby, but his only guards during his celebrations are the princesses. They are quick," Cassandra said. "But if you can grab Rapunzel's nose before they grab you, it will amplify your power, and you can defeat the king. Once he is dead, his power on this land will pass to the one who holds the crown. Since that will be you, then you can pass the crown to Baba, and she will begin the process of reversing the horrors the king has committed during his long reign."

I thought for a moment. "And what if I don't give the crown away?"

"Then Rapunzel will retract your blessing, and Baba will break you into a million pieces."

"Fair enough," I replied, leaning back. "I guess I will give Baba the crown then."

"See that you do, for all of our sakes." She looked at me one more time before closing her eyes. "Now, sleep."

CHAPTER 32
ROSE

I shouldn't have been surprised that Hypnos destroyed one of my favorite historic districts to build a series of casinos, cheesy even by Reno standards. After all, Hypnos long ago decided that anything old was disgusting, and that only new, sleek designs were worth anything. Still, I wept for the cute, cozy brownstones that made up the district, and the cobblestone streets that were demolished to create places like "Tex's Rootin' Tootin' Casino" and "Nero's Grotto," each announcing their existence through huge neon lights and loud music.

The minute we walked into Tex's, the sound accosted us. Whether it was dreamers laughing as they chugged pink cocktails, slot machines making ungodly blurts and beeps as people tossed dream orbs into them hoping for a jackpot, or the ambient music which bored into my brain, it was a lot to take in at once.

Lady Lynx scrunched her eyes against the lights and stepped carefully along the sticky red floors. She avoided a satyr shrieking after losing all their money on betting on double 00s on roulette, and a minotaur at the blackjack table yelling to double down.

Thick plumes of smoke settled over the tables in the poker section. People listlessly played the game at the outlying tables, but the action was concentrated on a large one in the center.

"There he is, I'm sorry to say," Lady Lynx whispered.

Hypnos sat behind a massive stack of chips. Around him sat an elf, a fairy, two dreamers, a gnome, a red cap, an owl, and a blue sylph.

"All in," Hypnos said, before his pink eyes found me. "Rose! What a wonderful surprise. I thought you were avoiding me."

"I'm not avoiding you. I was avoiding this place, though," I said, looking around. "I need to talk to you. Alone."

He studied his cards. "After this hand, though. I'm on a roll."

I groaned, but I didn't protest. The betting went around, and he won because it was his kingdom and he could win even without trying, though he'd say that he played everything straight. I didn't really care either way that he was lying to himself. I had long ago stopped trying to make Hypnos be a better god, content that he merely didn't run away.

He pulled his earnings and then told the table he was taking a break. He put on a pair of cheap sunglasses and led me to a table in the corner after Lady Lynx took her leave. He looked morose. "So, you need something, Rose? You know, you could just show up to say hi."

"This isn't really my scene, Hypnos. If you ever want to get some pizza, though, I'm there."

"I could make that happen right now, if you would like." He paused. "But I see from your eyes that you have something pressing to discuss. Has Chelle been kidnapped or something?"

"How did you—" I leaned in. "Did you have something to do with this?"

He laughed. "Of course not. I can't—you're not serious, are you? My gods you are. That is too rich."

I didn't find it funny. "She's been taken to the Celestial Realm, and I was told I need a full-blooded god to get inside to rescue her."

"You really shouldn't go there. The Celestial Realm is the worst. I know, I once lived there before my mother moved us here. It was simply awful."

"Be that as it may, I'm not going to let Chelle rot there in prison. Can you get me into the Celestial Realm or not?"

He raised his eyebrows. "Oh yeah, I can...I can, but I won't."

I scoffed. "Why don't you help me?"

"This may surprise you, but I'm not the best liked person at home. I made quite a few enemies in my day, and I have no interest in going back."

"You don't have to go back. Just get me there, then leave. I don't need you."

"Sorry, kid, but it's not going to happen. Why don't you talk to Persephone? I hear you two are tight now."

"I would rather not die, if I can help it."

"That's not the only way to find her. You could orgasm, for one. That's like a little death."

"Gross." I rolled my eyes. "Seriously with the—I saved all of Urgu, and you won't even bring me to the Celestial Realm?"

"How long will you skate by on that one accomplishment?" Hypnos asked. "You abandoned us right after, if I remember correctly, and then my mother ruined the Fates by letting one of my gorgons skitter away back to Earth to reunite with you."

"And if that gorgon dies, she'll never come back. What about that?"

"I guess that's a good point." Hypnos pursed his lips. "And I would bet that they brought my mother to the Crystal Keep, too, but no. I can't—really—I want to help you, but I can't leave all of this."

"This is, and I mean this from the bottom of my heart, complete and utter garbage." I slid my hand over his. "Please."

"I know what you want." His eyes found mine over the top of his glasses. "I'm not a hero."

"I'm not asking you to save her. I'm just asking you to give me the opportunity to do it."

"If you do this, you'll be on the run forever. There's nowhere in the universe you can hide from the Pantheon, and that's assuming you're successful. If you're not, you'll be tortured, or worse. Are you sure you know what you're doing?"

"Not at all, but I'm not going to leave Chelle to that place." I stood up. "I've had just about enough of convincing you. Either come with me now or go back to your stupid game. I know how important it is to you."

He sniffed and stood up with me. "Fine. After all, who knows what will happen if I let you go it alone. You'll make a deal for your soul, or something equally stupid if I'm not there to stop you."

I smiled. "Does that mean you're in?"

"Let me cash out my chips and I'll meet you at your apartment."

"Thank you."

He grunted. "Don't thank me. This is mind-numbingly stupid, and I shouldn't be enabling you."

"But you are, and I love you for it."

CHAPTER 33

CHELLE

"Move!" Athena shoved me, even though I was already going at a decent clip through the dark hallways beneath the Crystal Keep. The sting of the mixture we were bathed in still weighed heavily on my eyes, but at least I could see again, even if there was little more than darkness around us, and the glow from our restraints.

"You don't have to listen to them, you know," Nox said, as covered in glitter as me, and the target of even more ire from Athena. "They don't speak for all gods."

Athena cracked Nox in the back of the head with the butt of her laser cannon and sent the goddess of darkness careening off of the wall and onto the floor.

"You fool," Athena spat. "That's exactly what they do. Their will keeps the universe in balance, and safe from those that threaten it."

Nox managed to stand up and began walking again. "You are the foolish one to believe that. In all my years, I have only seen them make things better for themselves, with no measure of care for humanity, or even the other gods. Tell me, Athena, how has being the errand girl for a bunch of stuffy men made your life better?"

Athena went to smack Nox again, but when the goddess of darkness flinched, Athena stayed her hand. "Your contempt for the Board is what had led to your current situation. Perhaps it is best for you to close your mouth and learn your place."

"Why?" Nox's purple eyes began to glow. "Would they pity me then? Because I fell in line with their will? I don't want to live in a world like that."

"Then I have good news for you," Athena said with a dark smile. "Your fate will soon be decided."

Nox muttered under her breath and then went silent, marching along without giving Athena the satisfaction of another word. She listed to her right side as she moved, crashing into me every few steps, until I finally wrapped my arm around her to keep her straight.

"I'm sorry I got you into this," Nox whispered. "I know my fate already, but if I was not so arrogant, I could have spared you yours."

"Don't talk like that," I said. "You have a plan to get out of this, and we just have to follow it."

She shook her head. "I thought I would have time before Zeus took an interest in me. Apparently, I have become more of a thorn than I believed, especially after my stunt in the Fairy Realm."

Some months ago, Nox was responsible for reuniting the most powerful objects in the fae kingdom, the Xirgolov, and helping Unseelie fairies raise their Sunken Kingdom from a dark abyss that consumed their people. She'd gone against the gods' will to right that wrong, and my Rose was the champion she chose to deliver her justice.

"Will Rose be hurt for helping you?"

"I doubt it. She was nothing but a vessel, and the gods do not make a habit of punishing mortals. They believe that death is punishment enough and solves most of their problems."

"If she is hurt," I said, gritting my teeth, "I will be very put out."

"You'll be long since vaporized before they turn their attention to her, and your energy dispersed around the universe."

"That doesn't make me feel any better."

"Really?" Nox replied, dragging herself forward, wincing. "Finally finding peace doesn't give you some semblance of comfort? No Underworld. No afterlife, just the sweet silence of the abyss for the rest of eternity. Perhaps you have not seen enough to know what a gift nonexistence would be, but when you have seen as much as I have, the thought of simply not being is a comforting one."

"And yet, you fear what the Board will do to you."

"I do, because they will not do me the justice of blissful eternity."

"What will they do to you?" I asked.

"You were in the Dream Realm before the war, so I must assume you interacted with the gods Anansi, Hera, Sekhmet, Agrona, and Loki?"

"I've had my run-ins with them, yes."

She took a deep breath and winced in pain. "They were not the full incarnation of the gods. They were simply the souls, the troublesome part of them that caused such chaos they could no longer be trusted. Their souls were taken from their bodies and jailed in the Dream Realm, while their bodies—their bodies became nothing but hollow vessels, the perfect soldiers to carry out the Board's vision; brutal, powerful, and without a will of their own."

"That's horrible," I said. "I hate Hera, but to think of her body used against her will by the Board is vile."

"That will be my fate, too. If Osiris and the others have their way, eventually, it would be the fate of every god. Free will is a curse they have regretted since the beginning."

"No," I said. "I won't let that happen to you."

Nox chuckled and touched my cheek softly. "You're a sweet kid."

"No touching!" Athena said, rushing forward to pull us apart. "We're almost there. Just behave, all right?"

"Will that make them go easier on us?" Nox asked. A pinprick of light appeared in the distance.

"No," Athena replied. "But it will make me go easier on you, and I can still do a lot of damage before we reach them."

Nox smirked, biting her lip. There was a wild vengeful rage in her eyes, but she simply straightened herself and turned forward.

"Good girl," Athena growled. We continued along through the dark.

CHAPTER 34

RED

The first glass of cold honey wine coated my throat and restored my fortitude. The second bolstered my spirits. By the third, I was quite drunk.

"It's not often a mortal can keep up with the gods," Rama said with a smile, refilling my glass.

"I'm not quite a mortal, am I?" I replied. "I'm some sort of bastardized construction of the gods."

"Hey," Rama spoke firmly, stopping his drink before it reached his mouth. "What you are is unique among the realms of man and gods, and it's exactly that uniqueness that is incredibly valuable to our cause."

I slid closer to him. The honey wine humming from his breath made me smile as it mixed with the sweet scent of his cologne. "And what is your cause?"

Rama's eyes darted left and right, more out of habit than fear, before he turned back to me. "Why, to destroy the patriarchy and dismantle the Board of Directors, of course. I thought that would have been obvious."

"I love it!" I slammed my hand on the table, unable to

contain my laughter. "That is a tall order, though. Isn't the Board filled with the most powerful gods in the universe?"

"Maybe in sheer strength, but they are ill-equipped for the changing times, and we believe we should be led by other, more capable gods that better reflect our values."

"And what makes yours the right values?" I said, turning myself so I was nearly on top of Rama. "How are you not just another man, trying to impose his will on the universe?"

Now it was his turn to chuckle. He took an uncomfortable drink from his cup and answered, "That's part of it, maybe, but have you seen your world lately? Or my many worlds? The humans who inhabit them...they are not happy. They drift about their lives in pain, and that's the luckiest of them. Most drift through robotically, and do you know why that is?"

"Because existence is horrid?" I asked, catching my wobbling body.

"Well, yes, but do you know why that is?" When I simply shrugged, he continued. "Because the Board values strength above all else, and the will to impose one's values on another. They endow these people—these horrible people—bless them into power, all over the universe. And it ruins everything. These people, the ones who run your planet and mine, they are the worst kind of people, but the Board is enamored with them. It's not right. A new group of leaders would change the outcome of every planet in the cosmos."

"So, you're saying the reason that my planet, your planet, and every planet is so messed up is because the Board decides who to champion, and gives them the will to rule?"

Rama nodded, taking another sip of his honey wine. "Have you ever heard of divine right to rule? It's a concept that Zeus and Osiris championed. It led to thousands of countless wars with billions, trillions, of unnecessary deaths, and while that concept has fallen away in recent centuries, on most developed planets, the gods still carry it with them."

"Like when Rose was given Hypnos's blessing?" I asked.

He nodded again. "To an extent, but much smaller; an almost imperceptible hand that they place on the scales of certain people, who seem to luck themselves into power. I have tried to rail against it where I can, but the will of the Board is nearly absolute."

I finished my drink and took a drink from Rama's. "If they're a board, then you should just be able to vote them out, right?"

He snorted. "Tell me, have you ever seen a true democracy?"

I thought for a minute, but I hadn't. Even the United States of America, touted as the greatest democracy in the world, was a barely functioning one. "Not a good one, at least not for the long haul. Even if they start with good intentions, those intentions get corrupted by evil men."

"Exactly. Because rulers want to continue to rule, including here," Rama finished, before recovering his drink from my clutches. "And that truth traces itself back all the way to the Board. Every vote keeps them in power, no matter how many rally against them. Every coup ends with its conspirators dead. Every chance to wrest back power is squelched before it can gather steam. That's why saving Nox is so important."

"I don't follow."

"Because she is the head of our effort. She has moved in the darkness for eons, nudging the pieces in just the right place, and giving up the trump cards we need to finally beat the Board."

"What cards are those?"

He pointed at me. "You and Chelle."

"What?" I nearly spit out the sip I'd taken from his drink. "I'm no trump card. I'm just a silly girl from the Dream Realm who lucked into a body."

"No," Rama replied. "You're wrong. You and Chelle are the keys to all of this, which is why the Board will do anything to make sure you die, and that Nox is punished for creating you."

"But Nox didn't make me. Hypnos did."

"Yes, you have said that." He smiled. "And who do you think gave him that idea?"

The pieces connected then. Hypnos hated the idea of making me, and I had been told multiple times he would never do it again. It made sense that the reason he turned me was because of a suggestion from his mother.

"I don't know how I feel about being made a part of this without my knowledge or permission."

"Are you saying you don't want to topple the Board?" Rama asked, finishing his glass.

"Well, no. If what you're saying is true, and we can change everything by ousting the board, then I am willing to help. It just would have been nice to be asked."

"Gods aren't known for asking, but I will take it under advisement." He smiled at me, and his bright white teeth gleamed so brightly they nearly took my breath away. "Are you ready to save the universe, then?"

I thought for a second, then shrugged. "I have nothing better to do."

But that wasn't true. The better thing I had to do was pass out. As everything turned black, I smiled, because I couldn't remember the last time I'd slept. I hoped it was filled with good dreams.

CHAPTER 35
ARIEL

The memories, a thousand flashes of light, passed by me at once, traveling so fast I couldn't understand any of them. I clasped my hand around one and found myself bolting through the air, unable to stop. Inky blackness surrounded me, save for the light of the memories.

Wind pounded against my face and opening my mouth to take a breath only made me choke so violently that I let go of the memory out of pure instinct. I realized my mistake and reached for it again, but it was too late. The memory was out of sight.

I fell, grasping at the memories as they shot past me, cutting through my fingers, while my body plummeted towards the murky distance below me. I smashed into the ground, and it caught me like a vat of goo, taking me inside itself, halting my momentum, and spitting me out onto the obsidian glass of its surface.

I pressed my hands against my chest, trying to still my heart and regain control over my frantic breath. When I did, I saw the visage of a woman familiar to me from a time long past.

"Hello, Ariel," the woman said. "It's so nice to see you again."

"Mom?" I replied, confused. She wore a shimmering blue gown the color of the sea after a storm, with glittering beads that shone like the sun reflecting off the surface of the ocean. Her crown stood tall on her head, rose gold and beset with jewels on each of its ten points.

I always thought it would be hard to keep my thin neck steady under the weight of it all. However, my mother assured me that when it was time to wear the crown, it would be as light as a feather to me. That time never came, though. She died, and I was thrown to Ursula under the sea.

"The last time I saw you, they were dragging you from our carriage." My eyes were glassy. "Is it truly you?"

Her lip twitched, nearly into a smile. "A memory of the woman you knew, to comfort and guide you to the truth, and help you regain what was lost."

I shook my head. "I don't understand. Why would Nox and Ursula conspire to keep my memories from me?"

"One thing you learn, when you are as old as me, is that some things are not meant to be explained. They just are, and that has to be enough."

I frowned. "No, I don't accept that. I'm older now than you were after you died, and I have never thought that, for one moment, in my whole life. Why did you lock these memories from me? They are my memories. I have a right to know."

She stroked her chin. "When I was named as the ruler of the Land of Oz, I was given a secret, one that had been carried by my predecessors, one that stayed with me when I died, until this moment. Millennia ago, one of our kind flew too close to the sun in an attempt to gain the power of the gods. Her name was that of legend, but that legend ends before her true story begins. In punishment for her impu-dence, the gods tried to destroy her, but she had flown close enough to become the same immortal beings as they were —even worse, some would say. They tried to wrench her soul from her body, but she had found a way to prevent them from even that punishment. They had only one course of action left. They removed from her the source of her power: her eyes, her mouth, her nose, and her ears, and bound her to a planet so horrible that even the gods dare not speak its name. As for the pieces of her face, they cast them to the most loyal gods in the cosmos, giving the nose to the King in Yellow, who ruled Carcosa, the capital of their haunted world. They gave an ear to Hades, and another to Hel, ruler of the Underworld. The mouth they kept for themselves, hidden in the Celestial Realm. The eyes, they were given to Nox for safe keeping, hidden in the most secret places in the Dream Realm. That is the secret I carried and had given to you when you were named my successor. It is a secret that died with me, and lives in you. The final resting place of the left eye."

"The eye!" I shouted. "That's what Queen Aine wanted to know. Where is it? Tell me so that I might find it."

She shook her head. "I'm afraid it's not as easy as all that. This is the first step to unlocking me to guide you, but Nox buried the secret deep, in places only your soul may plunge. To find the next clue, you must travel beyond the palace, beyond the coral walls, and to the abandoned ship that lays beyond. I have left the next hint there."

My memory cleared, and I saw a dozen journeys to that ship over my years, always stopped by Cefus, or one of Ursula's men, before I could enter it.

"In the cabin of the ship, under the boards where there was once a bed, lies a box. Inside it, you will find the clue that will help you continue your journey." She reached forward and cupped my face in her hands. "You were the great joy of my life. Now, good luck to you, my love. The path you walk is perilous, and should the Faceless Woman regain her visage, the damage she could wreak on the universe is unfathomable." She reached forward and kissed my forehead. "Now go."

And with that kiss, my eyes went white. I bolted up in my bed in the bottom of the sea, with another piece of the puzzle unlocked, and an ominous portent of things to come.

The long, dark corridor under the Crystal Keep finally dead-ended at the stairwell to a large, circular chamber.. On each of six edges of the chamber stood granite statues a dozen feet tall, pointing ominously down at the place where we entered the room.

"Subtle," I muttered.

Along the floor, a mosaic depicted hundreds of humans of all types, colors, and shapes, screaming up at the gods for relief, and on the ceiling hundreds of gods mocked them from the heights of Heaven, refusing their pleas.

"The judgement of man," Athena said. "As you can expect, your kind has been found wanting."

"I'm only half human," I shot back. "The other half you cursed, remember?"

"It wasn't a curse; it was a gift. A gift that you squandered."

"Whatever."

She pushed me towards a red-lacquered door that dwarfed the statues around it. Depictions of the six granite gods spread out in gold relief on its surface, mixed with flowers and other symbolism from the ancient Greek, Egyptian, and Norse that I'd picked up on my travels, along with several others that I couldn't place.

Athena dropped to her knee on a blooming rose mosaic. When her knee touched the ground, it glowed a haunting blue. "Your graces, I have brought the sinners for your reprisal."

A shock rippled through my body and forced me to the ground. Nox was equally prostrate on her knees, and my head bent down until it touched the ground. The same happened to Nox. The same blue glow emanated under me, and the door cracked open, sliding along with great effort.

"Let's go," Athena said, lifting Nox to her feet with one hand and me with the other. She shoved us through the door. Lights clicked on from overhead, guiding us past more stone reliefs of the gods and monsters of legend. I paused to study a great screaming gorgon being slaughtered by Perseus, and I sneered at the sheer audacity of it.

"It's weird that so much of mythology came from Earth," I said.

Athena scoffed. "You humans are so arrogant. Those stories don't come from Earth. They were brought there, just as they are brought to every planet in the universe. The universe does not rotate around you. It, in fact, rotates around this very room."

We continued until I reached a ledge guarded by a handrail. Athena pushed me down into a leather padded kneeler. When my hands touched the railing, my shackles magnetized to it, preventing me from moving, and did the same with my legs.

"Nox," a voice boomed. "So nice of you to grace us with your presence." A light shone down from the other side of the room to reveal a large, bearded man with a tunic covering his broad chest and shoulders and a wreath of holly around his head.

"How could I not, when you came so far to retrieve me, Zeus?"

"How do you expect us to behave?" another voice sounded, next to Zeus. Another light shone down on a dark-skinned man with a long, thin tuft of hair coming from the middle of his chin, wrapped in gold. He wore thick eyeliner that curled like a cat's tail on the edges of his face. The rest of his head was bald, and the light bounced off it. "When you betray us so openly."

"It was never my intention to betray you, Osiris," Nox said.

"Then why am I looking at this abomination against our will?" A third light turned on to show us a tired-looking man with a black beard fraying in every direction, and with a dozen layers to it. The gold band around his head kept his long hair out of his eyes.

A fourth light flicked on to reveal another white man, not unlike the last, except he had no beard but a mustache that came down to his chin. His facial hair compensated for the hair thinning on the top of his head.

"And what is this we have heard about using the Xirgolov to raise the Sunken Kingdom, after we expressly forbade such a thing?"

"We made a mistake, Ukko." Nox directed her attention to the fourth god revealed. "I didn't raise a finger to help. I only guided my chosen champion in the right direction. You have all done as much in your long lives, have you not?"

"And what of this girl?" the black-haired god asked, raising a finger towards me.

Nox lowered her head. "That is another matter, Svarog.

I admit to granting her as a boon to my chosen champion for success in her adventure, as written into law."

Another light flicked on. Under it sat a man with three heads, each more beautiful than the last. They each looked at Nox, and then spoke in unison. "You know that bringing a soul back from the dead is the cardinal sin of our people."

"And yet, Brahma," Nox said, "you must admit to doing the same."

"To children shortly dead, and to champions that cling to life. Not to souls long dead, with no bodies to call their own."

"Splitting hairs, I think. Hardly enough to warrant such an effort on your part." Nox was calm. She cleared her throat. "Why don't you admit why you have really brought me here? To wrest control of the Dream Realm from my hands."

"Pathetic." The final light went on, and under it sat a dark gray man with a strong jaw. He wore little except for a shawl around his shoulders, and a high black hat with no brim. "We have no interest in your realm, Nox."

"You have always wanted to control it, Tengri." She glared at him. "You, specifically. You can't stand that I have something you can't control. That's why you have always hated the other realms outside of this one, and now, you have brought me to a kangaroo court to take what I have built."

A gavel slammed down. Osiris held it in his hand. "Enough. You will have your chance to speak and plead your case."

"What is the point?" Nox said. "You have already made up your mind."

"If that were the case," one of Brahma's heads said. "You would already have been dealt with."

"We both know you couldn't just pull my soul from my body without some sham of a trial. There would be severe repercussions to such an act that even you aren't prepared to handle...yet." Nox rolled her eyes. "But please, let us get the charade started."

CHAPTER 37

NIMUE

"I was wondering when you would get here," the Faceless Woman said when I opened my eyes. She sat cross-legged. "Don't be afraid. This is a safe place to speak inside your dreams."

"Don't lie to me, Rapunzel. I know that nowhere with you is safe."

She had no face, even here in my dreams, but I still felt her smile. "Then you know my true name."

"I know what Cassandra told me, but she doesn't seem to know much."

"Because I have not told her much. I've told you more than any other, and if you bring me my nose, I will tell you everything. But for now, we have other matters to attend."

I sat down across from her. "You should know I don't like being jerked around."

"Yes," she replied. "Every time you have become powerful enough, you have killed those who, as you said, jerked you around. I have no intention of doing that, but please believe that even if I did, you would never become powerful enough to kill me. Not even the gods could do so. Believe me, they tried."

"I've heard that before, my whole life, and yet I'm the one still alive."

She cocked her head. "The way you speak... We are not enemies, are we?"

"No," I said. "I very much want to learn from you, but I want to be clear that I am not your puppet. I expect a return on my suffering, ten-fold."

"A hundred-fold," she replied. "That is my promise to you, if you succeed where so many have failed."

"How many have you sent to their deaths?"

She shook her head. "Not death. Much worse than death, which is why I have come to you now, to show you how to defeat the king. You only have an instant, and you must be precise."

"Tell me," I said, leaning forward.

"At the opening night reception, the king will welcome every guest with a handshake. He will wear his finest garb, and his prized possession, my nose, will be on display around his neck to prove that he is more powerful than even his most feared enemy."

"He isn't though, right?"

"No, but he needs people to believe he is, so that they cower in fear from him. When it comes to your turn, you must grab the nose with your left hand, and then touch his wrist with your right. He will be protected save for the gloves he wears have an opening under his palm where it connects to his bracers. You must grab them both at the same time. Otherwise, the guards will be on you, and you will have failed. Understand?"

I nodded. "I understand."

"When you touch him, you will have the ability to do

anything you wish to him in that instant. That's when you must slit his head from his body, and have it roll to your feet. Pick up the nose and call me to you. I will handle the rest."

A disturbing thought passed through me. "Cassandra? Did she try, and fail?"

Rapunzel nodded. "She was young and naïve. She held great promise but look at what happened to her. The king is old and wily. He has ruled for a long time because he trusts nothing. Do not underestimate him."

"I won't," I said. "I've dealt with his kind before. In another world, I might say he was a man after my own heart."

"I'm counting on that fact, actually." Rapunzel touched my forehead. "Your instinct to survive is your secret weapon. Use it."

CHAPTER 38
ARIEL

Memories of my previous trips past the coral wall came back to me as I swam through the crack in its border. On every one of my other trips through the barrier, I thought I'd found some undiscovered secret. The truth was, it was only new to me because my beloved mother Ursula wiped my memory each time "to protect me." For three hundred years.

She tried to stop me from leaving this time, too. I thought she might even send me to the dungeon under the castle, but then her face softened, and for a single, solitary moment, she looked like the mother I loved again; the one that protected me from the outside world and kept me safe…but that wasn't the truth, was it? She wasn't protecting me from the outside world. No, she was protecting the secrets in my head, like I was some locked box safe that Nox could hide under the floorboards.

"I don't like this, Princess," Cefus said. Mother wouldn't stop me from leaving, but she demanded I take Cefus "for my protection." What would an undersized servant do to protect me from the horrors of the deep? She sent him to keep an eye on me for her and make sure I didn't unlock any secrets that should stay buried.

"You've stopped me a dozen times over the centuries, Cefus. Don't pretend you aren't well acquainted with this ship."

"The outside of the ship, yes," he said. "But I have never been inside. I have heard tales that it is haunted."

I couldn't help but chuckle. "We are the haunted, Cefus. We don't have bodies. We are nothing but souls floating through space! This whole continent is haunted."

"I hadn't thought of that." Cefus frowned. "Now, I am even more glad that I live under the sea."

If he was trying to convince me that my life under the sea was something to be envied, he was failing. The moment that Ursula unlocked my memories, the sea was dead to me. I wanted nothing more to do with it. For so long the cold of its water wrapped me in a cocoon; one I thought protected instead of stifled, but now I knew the truth. Nothing but the thought of a jail cell held me back from broadcasting it.

"*Lux*," I muttered, and a small light rose from my hands, illuminating the way. In all my years trying to find this ship, of being pulled inexorably towards it, I had never even once swam through the cracks in the rotten wood, so my heart leapt as I crossed the precipice of the hull.

It was remarkably well-preserved, but then again, so was I. The wood was warped, certainly, and worn with time, but there was more damage from the kelp, coral, and other denizens that had reclaimed the ship for themselves than from the water. I snaked my way through the galley, where small fish fluttered through the cabinets.

"I don't like this place," Cefus muttered, but it drew no sympathy from me.

They weren't ghosts, per se, but when I turned my head too fast, I swore I saw the flickering of a memory, people eating at the mess hall tables, or walking between the cabins. When Cefus's complaints fell silent, I could even make out the sounds of utensils clacking together, and the robust laughter of the people who roamed the ship's halls.

What had happened to them when the ship fell under the sea? The mermaids were not as kind to them as I was, I would bet, but when I asked Ursula, she just looked away, and Cefus would never tell me anything that hadn't come from the queen's mouth.

My mother, my real mother would have—no, that was not true. She was no more my mother than Ursula. She was just a woman who treated me with kindness, and who I imprinted on since she'd shown me an ounce of respect, and in that moment a horrible thought crossed through my mind. What if my mother, the one who raised me to be queen, had brought me up with some sort of purpose, like my adopted mother had, and this was all a part of her sick game?

They'd both had a part in sealing my fate, and my memories, after all, which was such a violation I couldn't even wrap my brain around it. I wanted my memories back. I wanted to know the truth, even if it was manufactured by the people who I thought loved me most.

I pulled myself through the mess hall, with its long wooden tables strewn about the room, and up towards the quarters at the front of the ship. The crew must have occupied the first few I passed, with dozens of bunk beds lying about haphazardly, but the quarters became more ostentatious, and I started to hear a distinct hum that grew louder as I approached.

"Do you hear that?" I called back to Cefus.

"I'm trying very hard not to hear anything, ma'am."

I pulled myself into a small cabin. It was beautiful, even in its derelict condition, but it would have been grand when it was new. A four-poster bed, broken and cracked, was toppled over and leaned against the far wall along with a chest of drawers and a cracked mirror. I scanned the room, taking in the trinkets and photos, undisturbed even after so many years. but that wasn't what caught my attention.

There was a soft glow under the floorboards. I pressed my hand down and the wood gave, breaking in half with almost no pressure. Underneath, just as my mother said, was a golden box, inlaid with ivory and silver. I pulled it to my chest.

My whole body glowed a brilliant golden hue like the box, which clicked open. Inside laid a key, ornate and embossed with a silver rose. Six jewels of different types were embedded into the tip of the key in a circle, and I knew immediately that it was a mark of the Church of the Six.

It was a clue, and a direction, but I had hoped for more. I had hoped another flood of memories might be unlocked. Instead, I was still adrift in an ocean with more questions than answers.

CHAPTER 39

ROSE

I woke up with a nice, long cat stretch. I always felt better after drifting into the Dream Realm. The place unsettled Chelle, and she woke from her trips more drained than when she went to bed. She hated it so much that I would wake up cheery and ready for the day when she could barely drag her head off the pillow. Maybe it's because Hypnos's blessing flowed through me when I was in Urgu, and I always woke feeling my most powerful, like I could conquer anything.

I rolled out of bed and rubbed the sleep from my eyes. After putting on my slippers, I heard Jamil playing with Cheyenne in the other room. I walked out the door towards the kitchen just as Cheyenne shouted a big "aroo" into the air and dove for a stuffed monkey. She had long ago chewed off its arms and legs and punctured the squeaker, but whenever I tried to give her another one, she wouldn't even look at it.

"Thanks for watching her," I said to Jamil, kneeling to scritch Cheyenne's neck as she leapt towards me with half her body wagging in excitement to see me.

"My pleasure," Jamil said. "Any luck?"

I shrugged. "He said yes, but Hypnos is not the most reliable god. If he doesn't show up, I'll just have to find somebody else. Maybe Persephone. She owes me about a hundred favors." I opened the junk drawer where I kept the godcoin that Hypnos had given me. I really didn't want to travel into the Underworld again, but if that's what it took to—

As I rubbed the coin in my fingers, a brilliant white light cut across the room, starting as a sliver on the ceiling, then splitting down the sides. A door appeared in the middle of my living room.

"Oh good, it worked." Hypnos pulled off his sunglasses and placed them in his pocket, his pink eyes glowing even brighter than the door he emerged from. "The last one opened in the middle of the Pacific."

He noticed the large puddle of water he'd brought in with him and flinched in shame, an emotion I didn't think he had, and raised his hand, pulling all the water away. Then he looked down at Cheyenne, who had hopped forward and was dancing in the air for some pets.

"Weird," I said. "She doesn't like anyone."

He scritched Cheyenne under the chin, and she nuzzled into him. "Dogs love me. Always have. She's a cutie." His face turned down. "Plagued by nightmares though, and a lot of anxiety." He placed his hands on her cheeks and for a moment her little eyes glowed pink. "That should help."

Cheyenne tumbled onto the ground and licked his fingers as he continued petting her.

"What did you do to her?" I asked.

"Nothing big, just helped unblock a part of her that prevented her from having good dreams. Also, corrected a melatonin deficiency that stopped her from going to sleep at all. She should be much happier now."

I blinked, baffled. "Thank you."

"Least you could do," Jamil growled.

Hypnos looked over at her and faked a smile. "Ah, my wood nymph friend. How did you do in Reno?"

"Won a couple grand and took all your winnings and blew them on—well, what happens in Reno stays in Reno."

"I don't think that's the expression," I said, rubbing Cheyenne's belly.

"It's my expression," Jamil said. "And if you want me to watch that dog, just let me have this one."

"If you insist." I shrugged. "Thank you, by the way."

"Are you kidding? A vacation in New York City on your dime. You're almost doing me a favor."

I picked Cheyenne up and hugged her. She must have known something was happening, because she shivered in my arms and looked at me with her big, wet, blue eyes. We hadn't been apart from each other for more than a night since I found her wandering the streets aimlessly and brought her home. She looked far less pathetic now than she did waterlogged with clumps of dirt stuck to her hair.

"It's going to be okay, girl," I said. "Jamil is good people, and I'm going to bring back Mommy, and we'll be a family again." At the word 'mommy' her tail wagged furiously. "Yeah, you love Mommy, right?" She licked my nose. "Okay, girl. I love you."

"We really should go," Hypnos said. "If I know the Board, they've probably already started their mockery of a trial."

I nodded and placed Cheyenne in Jamil's arms. "Be good, okay?"

"I'm always good," Jamil answered.

"I was talking to the dog." I pulled out my credit card and handed it to her. "Whatever you need, okay?"

"Got it. New Tesla, here we come."

"Need," I said. "Not want. *Need.*"

"I have expensive needs." She cracked a coy smile. "I'm kidding. Go, it will all be fine."

I took one last look back at Cheyenne crying out for me to stay, and a tear rolled down my cheek as I grabbed Hypnos's hand and disappeared into the nothingness. When we reappeared in the Dream Realm, in front of the Obsidian Spindle, my resolve congealed again. *I am doing this for Chelle, and nothing will stop me from bringing her home.*

"You ready?" Hypnos didn't wait for me to reply before answering his own question. "No, you're not ready. Trust me."

"I've been all over the known universe. I think I'll be fine."

He pulled a key off his neck and stuck it into the lock of the Spindle. Instead of opening, the door turned white. "That's the spirit. That kind of optimism is completely misplaced, but I'm glad you have it."

We disappeared once again into the unknown. It happened so often to me that I was surprised when the familiar prick of fear knotted in my stomach.

CHAPTER 40

RED

Ow, I thought as I moved my head from the pillow. I was a force of god energy, and I had a massive hangover. I had never had a hangover in my hundreds of years in the Dream Realm and died before I had my first sip of alcohol, so the splitting in my head was something I only knew from stories.

"Oh good," Rama said, rolling over in bed towards me. "You're up."

I leapt from the bed before he could wrap his arm around me, disgust shooting down my spine. "My gods. You didn't—we didn't—did we?"

He threw his head back and laughed. "Woman, you are still wearing your linens. If I ravished you, I guarantee you would be naked as a jaybird."

I was, in fact, still clothed, save for my cape and weapons on the nightstand. "Why were you lying with me, then?"

"Ha!" He cackled in delight. "You literally pulled me into bed when I tried to put you here and yelled at me when I tried to leave. It has been a long time since I slept, and it felt…oddly refreshing." He leapt out of bed, buck naked. "But we now have business to attend."

"My gods, man!" I screamed, averting my eyes. "You're naked."

"Of course I am." He slipped his pants back on. "Does it offend you to see a perfect specimen in the flesh?"

"No…it's just been a long time. And besides, it's not proper."

"Woman, the things you said to me as I laid you in bed were not proper either, but I do not hold them against you."

It wouldn't be the gods that struck me down here in the Celestial Realm, or even an errant arrow, but embarrassment. Mercifully, Rama finished changing and slid past me without another word. I readied myself for battle and headed down the stairs.

"And here she is, the woman of the hour," Rama called out, presenting me like a prized pig to a panel of judges. "Everyone, meet Gabrielle, the Red Rider."

"She doesn't look like much," a stocky woman said with a grunt. "What does she ride?"

"Easy, Aditi," Rama said. "She's not the enemy here."

"No," a tall slender woman said, wearing a golden dress and green beret. "But if we are to put our faith in her, we deserve to know she's up to the task."

"And you shall, Hepit—"

"I don't have to prove myself to anyone," I snapped. "I have come to save my friend, with or without you. Saving Nox is ancillary to that cause. If you want to join with me, then I ask what right you have to judge me, when I should be the one casting my eyes on you."

The final member of their party, a dark-skinned woman wearing no fewer than ten thick golden necklaces and the tattoo of stars on each cheek, smiled. "I like her."

"I knew you would, iNyanga," Rama said, pulling me forward. "She has a fire in her belly which is, frankly, refreshing after dealing with you dullards for a century."

"Watch it," Hepit said. "You're the only man in this operation, and I have no problem turning you into worse if you keep up with the lip."

"Would you stop yapping and tell me what's going on!" I shouted, stomping my foot to try and get some measly amount of attention from them. That's when I noticed that the bar, which was bustling earlier, was empty except for the five of us. "Who are all of you?"

"The Circle of Truth," Aditi replied. "I thought Rama would have at least told you that."

Another wave of pain crackled in my head, and iNyanga guided me towards the bar. "Who knows what Rama told you with all that alcohol coursing through you." She snapped her fingers and a green lion appeared wearing a jaunty suit and slid a green mixture towards us. "Drink this. It will help."

As I downed the drink and the fuzziness in my head cleared, Hepit slid up next to me. "For generations, the Board has held a tyrannical grasp on the Celestial Realm. We aim to bring them down a peg, and then disband them all together."

I slammed the finished drink glass on the table. "And part of that involves Nox."

"She is the key to it all." Adita nodded solemnly. "Without her, we fall apart, and the Board knows that. They have tried to place her under arrest for eons, but nothing stuck until she helped raise the Sunken Kingdom."

"I see," I said. "And how do I fit into this plan?"

"Quite well," Rama said. "You are very special. Powerful enough to survive entering the Crystal Keep, but weak enough to avoid detection by the sentries. You can sneak in, save Nox, rescue your friend, and escape before anyone knows better."

"If that's the case," I replied, "then I think you should be a little bit nicer to me."

"We wi—"

A bell sounded in the room, and everybody stood at attention, darting their eyes back and forth between each other. A few seconds later, the sound of footsteps echoed in the hallway, and then two figures entered the room.

"Rose?" I asked. "Hypnos?"

"My gods!" Rose shouted, running towards me. "I never thought I would see you again."

"What are you doing here, Hypnos?" Rama replied. "How did you know about this place?"

"My mother was captured, and I thought the least I could do on my way through the Celestial Realm to rescue her was pay a visit to the group of reckless psychos responsible for her capture."

"We had nothing to do wi—" Hepit started, but Hypnos held up his hand.

"I don't care, as long as you help me get her out, and the little gorgon girl she's with."

Rama smiled. "For once, Hypnos, I think our goals are aligned."

CHAPTER 41
ARIEL

No one from the Emerald City greeted me when I stepped back onto land. Cefus begged me to return to the castle instead of going to the surface where he couldn't protect me, but I abandoned him, refusing to be a prisoner in my own life anymore. I spoke the words he'd taught me, and by the time I reached the road, I was halfway presentable, hair and clothes dry, my face looking only half a waterlogged fright.

It was a long walk to the Emerald City, and while I was determined to make it there by myself, I was grateful when a kindly driver stopped his horseless carriage to offer me a ride. It wasn't quite as nice as the limo, but it had conditioned air which wrapped around me like the cold of the sea.

"Where are you from?" he asked. There was a twang in his accent I never heard before.

"The bottom of the sea," I replied, matter of fact, only realizing that it was odd after his face dropped. "They call me the Drowned Princess, but that's silly because a soul cannot drown."

"I'm from Texas. That's in America. Or I was, 'til my body crapped out on me one night."

"Crapped out?" My head cocked. "What does this mean?"

"Oh, yeah, I forgot some of you are from like, forever ago. It means I died in my sleep."

"Ah, I did the same."

Our conversation was stilted, but I learned that he was on his way to the Emerald City on business, and that he traveled all over Urgu, except the Mistreach, selling something called vacuum cleaners. He said they helped people suck up dirt from their homes to keep them clean, which I found silly because magic existed to do those sorts of things.

There was a no carriage rule, horseless or otherwise, within a mile of the castle, so he said goodbye and dropped me off a ways away. I set off in the direction of the castle but was headed to the building right next to it, The Cathedral of the Six. There, I hoped to unlock the secrets in my brain.

Though they were hazy, I had a few memories of the Cathedral. The stained glass I remembered being more magnificent and varied in its depictions of the gods. While Hera, Anansi, Loki and Sekhmet, were still pictured, Agrona was absent, replaced by Nox, and Hypnos's visage was ever more present than before.

Nox had told me stories about the glorious deaths of Hera, Anansi, and Sekhmet in defense of the realm, how Agrona had betrayed them, and how only Loki lived, a husk of his former glory, hidden in the bogs and marshes common in the Southwest of Urgu.

Before the war, Nox had remained hidden from those in the realm; for eons none saw her except those working in the background. But after, she had no choice but to make herself known to the whole of Urgu in order to save it from certain destruction. It felt strange to see her shining through the stained glass as I walked into the magnificent cathedral, as I knew she preferred the shadows.

"Many blessings to you, traveler," a black-suited deacon's voice echoed down the pews.

It was relatively empty, but a few people speckled the pews and altars, lighting candles to the Six in the alcoves devoted to them and praying for a blessing. Little did they know that a god's blessing brought only pain and heartbreak, even if it offered extraordinary power.

"Good evening, Father," I replied, bowing my head.

He waved a hand in the air. "None of that, please. I am but a humble friar of the order. How may we help you today?"

"I'm looking for Cardinal Edwina. Do you know her?"

He winced. "Unfortunately, the cardinal was summarily dusted when she led a coup against Queen Rose. Nasty business. Did you know the cardinal?"

"Very well. She was present at my mother—at the coronation of the queen when I was young to this place. How horrible that she would do that to one of Hypnos's chosen."

"Yes, it was a blight on the church. We have moved on from her memory, though we honor the good in her." He looked at me closely. "If you knew her that long ago, then you must be hundreds of years old."

I nodded. "Older than I would like to admit." I pulled the key from my hand and showed it to him. "Do you by chance know of this key?"

The deacon took it and turned it over in his hand. "I have never seen its equal. Come, I will bring you to the oldest monk in the order. They are busy writing this week's sermon but would be happy to meet with one such as you."

We reached the end of a wood-paneled hallway, and he knocked on a thick, oak door. I wasn't expecting the young voice welcoming us. When we entered the room, I saw a child no more than ten, sitting cross-legged in a miniature robe, a bald spot carved into her small head.

"Good evening, deacon," she said with a smile. "How may I help you?"

I did my best to hide my wonder. When I walked the surface, I often met those older than me who still appeared to be children, but I had not seen one in so long that I feared that my astonishment showed on my face.

"This woman has a question about this key." He handed it to the girl, who studied it closely. "Do you know anything about it?"

"Of course," she said, turning to me. "Welcome home, Ariel. It has been a long time since I have seen you. Please sit." Her eyes moved back to the deacon. "Thank you, Thomas. Now, please leave us."

He bowed his head as he walked away. "Of course, Mother Rebecca."

When the door closed, Rebecca tilted her head towards me. "How are you finding the surface?"

"It's fine. People are nice. A bit warmer than I would like, and I miss floating, but it's fine."

She held up the key. "If you have this, then your memories must have returned."

"Only partially," I said. "I'm hoping that key can unlock the rest of them, and remind me who I truly am."

"Your memories won't do that." She touched my chest with her delicate hand. "Who you are is in here, and that can never be taken from you."

"That's a nice sentiment, but I would like my memories back all the same."

She smiled again, gently. "Of course. You are lucky that the tabernacle was not destroyed with the rest of the Cathedral in the Great War. Otherwise, this might have been lost."

She pulled out a thin folded cloth from inside of an old book and unwrapped it gingerly with both hands. Inside was a dried orchid with six petals, representing the six gods of Urgu. It was the same type of petal my mother used to teach me about the gods when I first came to the Dream Realm. Immediately, I knew exactly where to go.

CHAPTER 42

ROSE

I couldn't believe Gabrielle was here, in living breathing color. It had been months since I'd seen her last, when she left to track down the Dark Planet and the wicked witch Nimue. I had tried to convince her to let it go; Nimue was gone, and the Spindle was destroyed, but she wouldn't hear it. Nimue had terrorized two realms, and almost brought a plague to Earth in the form of the Faceless Woman. She had to pay, so Red went after her.

I never thought I would see Red again, but here we were in the exact same place, in the same realm, halfway across the universe.

"It's good to see you," I said, sitting across from her at a table in the back of the strange bar. Hypnos was deep in conversation with the other gods, and they banished us to the kiddie table as they dealt with this wrinkle in their plan, the turn of fortune that brought us all together.

"There she is." I had opened Agent Edward's tracking device and tuned it to Chelle's frequency, only to see it blip. "She's here, and she's alive."

"That's wonderful! I could not be happier right now,"

Red replied. "Well, that's not true. Were Nimue dead and Chelle free, I would be happier. And if I were back on Earth."

I took a sip of tea that the green lion had brought over to me. "Yes, though, I am starting to lose my love for Earth. It has become a mess since you left, what with the revelation that magic exists."

"Really?" Red said, a bewildered look on her face. "Frankly, it was confusing to me that they didn't know already. We knew, and that was back hundreds of years ago. You would think with people taking selfies and videos of themselves all over the world they would have run into something."

I shrugged. "I'm sure they have, but distrust and misinformation are everywhere. Perhaps Mulder was right..." I waited for her to get my reference, but then realized she wouldn't have any reason to watch *The X Files*. "The truth is out there."

She nodded solemnly. "This Mulder seems wise. Is he a prophet I should know about?"

"Not quite." I laughed. "If we ever get back to Earth, we'll watch the show."

"I would like that."

"Be forewarned. It gets really, really gross."

"I have pulled out a man's intestines while he gasped for his last breath. I can handle gross."

"I guess you're right." I took another sip of my tea. "It used to gross me out, but now, with everything that's happened to me, I doubt I would even bat an eye, even at the flukeworm."

"Fluke...worm?" Red cocked her head, her eyebrows arched.

"Nothing," I replied, my eyes tracking over to the group

of gods circling each other across the room. "Do you know anything about their plan?"

"No." She bit her lip. "They were about to tell me when you walked in. If it's anything like the gods, it will be overly arrogant and riddled with flaws."

"Tell me how you really feel."

"I do not like the gods," Red replied, stone-faced. "Do you feel differently?"

I thought for a moment. "I'm not sure. They destroyed my life, but they have also helped me build a new one. Hypnos is selfish and vain, but he is risking himself to help me. Not to mention the likes of Anansi and Sehkmet, who died protecting us, and Persephone, who single handedly held back the divide to keep her people safe."

"And for every one of them, there are ten like Epiales working to unweave the threads of reality and bring chaos into the world. They are too powerful to exist."

I slid my hand over hers. "You wouldn't be here without Hypnos."

Before she could respond, the gods' conversation broke, and Rama called us over. Hepit slid a chair out from the table across from her, and iNyanga did the same, allowing us to sit with them.

"We're sorry for keeping you in the dark for so long," Aditi started, catching my eye. "Your presence brings some complications to our plan, but also betters our chances for success. We believed we would have to break into the boardroom and take Nox and Chelle from under the Board's nose, but with you both here," she pointed at me and then Hypnos, "we can use their own rules against them."

"Explain," Red said.

"Our informants have confirmed that Nox and Chelle are on trial for their very existence, which means we have precious little time. We have one trump card, though. Any relations to the incarcerated are allowed to meet with the prisoners, and then plead their case as character witnesses to the Board." She turned to Hypnos. "Your ability to petition the Board is assured, being as you are blood."

Rama looked at me intently. "Do you have any relation to the gorgon?"

"Besides her being the love of my life?"

"That's not good enough."

I looked down and twisted my ring. "We are...engaged."

It wasn't a lie. Not really. She was going to propose, and I still said yes, just not at the same time. Her asking formally was just a minor detail.

"That will have to be enough." Hepit stroked her chin. "I pray it is."

"Who does a god even pray to?" I asked.

"Ourselves, of course."

"And what will I do?" Red asked. "Twiddle my thumbs while Rose gets to have all the fun? Not that I'm complaining. It will be nice not to put myself on the line for once."

Aditi shook her head. "No, you have an incredibly important role. While the guards bring Nox and Chelle to their relations, you must break into the prison and unlock all the cells, causing a riot so that we will be able to steal away the prisoners."

"Oh," Red replied. "The most dangerous job is on me. That makes sense."

I squeezed Red's hand. "You don't have to do this. She isn't your fiancée."

"No, but she is yours, and you are both my friends. I won't let her rot in prison."

CHAPTER 43
NIMUE

I had been to enough formal events, between the Emerald Palace and around the little fiefdoms of Urgu, that I understood the procedure. The pomp and circumstance. As Queen of Oz, I often signed off on the plans. The Faceless Woman could not have chosen a better emissary for the task at hand, or perhaps she chose the task at hand to match the emissary. If I were an experienced courtesan, would she have instead chosen to have me seduce the king? Or if I was an expert baker, would I have been sent to poison his blood pudding?

It didn't matter. I was a queen, trained in the art of court politics. Every court was filled with minions, malcontents, and sycophants, hungry for power. Some plotted to steal it through deception, others worked to siphon it off through being as loyal as possible, while still others fell to their knees, in every respect, for a chance to win just a glimmer of it.

Cassandra brought us to a boarding house where we could change into the new gowns Rapunzel had commissioned to look our best for our presentation to the king. My dress was a glittering canary yellow with a deep slit in the center to accentuate the universe swirling in my chest. Cassandra wore a flowing gown of ivory and red that resembled blood pouring down from her neck.

The streets buzzed with the rumors of a new princess coming to the ball, and I felt the electricity in the air as I looked at the twisted black castle rising high above the city against the blood red sky.

"It has all come down to this," Cassandra said, stepping into the freshly washed carriage. The horses had been groomed and fed, and even the odd driver had on a tuxedo for the occasion.

When we were seated and the carriage lurched forward, Cassandra opened a small cupboard hidden in the door and pulled out two glasses, and then a carafe of dark black liquid.

"To our health," she said, taking a sip.

"To our success," I replied, before doing the same. The flavor was like black licorice tempered with gelatin, and its sticky heat coated my throat and stuck to my tongue. "What is this?"

"The king's touch is toxic, and foul. This will prevent it from having an effect on you. It is a vile but necessary component of court life."

Nearer to the castle, we fell in line behind a string of garish coaches, each fancier than the last, and I suddenly felt very self-conscious about ours, wondering whether we would be found as frauds before we even arrived.

"The court knows that I have been laid low," Cassandra said. "But they also know that I have a powerful ally to allow me to come here every year."

"Do they know it is Rapunzel?"

"They have their suspicions, but none have said so out

loud, and they dare not ask to my face for fear of her reprisal."

"So, even here, she is feared and respected."

"Many believe she will be the salvation of this place, while others would like nothing more than to eliminate her and any she associates with, in favor of the king."

"They all desire power. Some believe they will receive more with Rapunzel, while others lay their lot with the king, knowing their tenuous grasp on it will slip away should he be dethroned."

"Yes," Cassandra said with a slight nod. "They would rather live in fear of the horror they know than dream of a better world. The monster you know, after all, is better than the one you don't."

I couldn't help but laugh. "I had my share when I was queen. Those who would love to have seen me dusted into oblivion but feared what would happen when my replacement was crowned." I watched the procession inch forward. "When I was finally deposed, those loyal to me even went so far as to assassinate my replacement. They hated me, but they hated losing power more."

"Were you really so much of a monster?"

"Maybe not compared to your king, but yes, in some ways. Every ruler must be, to be effective, or die an idealist, like poor Rose. Besides, those that crave power have certain proclivities that allow them to achieve it, and they exist in me as they exist in all rulers, great or terrible."

Cassandra fell silent. Those who preferred comfortable lies to silence often had that response. They wanted to believe that there was a right and a wrong and evil could be defeated, not that it could only be supplanted with other evil. But anyone who sought out power was unworthy to wield it, whether it was me, the Faceless Woman, or Cassandra's precious Baba.

Those who sought power knew that truth, and that the only way to protect yourself was to acquire more power, in a never-ending arms race. I tried once to believe that I could be a nothing; that I could stay out of the fray, that power was an evil I didn't have to chase, and in that time, I was walked all over, humiliated, and treated like a cad. *Never again.*

It took over an hour to reach the front of the line, and when we did, a four-eyed woman with skin as black as onyx opened the door for us. Up close, the castle was not the ominous, imposing thing I'd seen from the window of the boarding house. Even magic couldn't hide the cracks in the façade, and the broken wings of the gargoyles perched around the grounds, hollow-eyed, screaming out into the nothing.

The caws of crows echoed above us as all manner of horror walked into the castle, streaming from their cabs in elegant robes and stately dresses.

"Are you ready?" Cassandra asked, offering me her arm.

"Whether I am or not, it's time to end this, one way or another."

And we started inside, with the fate of the Dark Planet resting heavy on our shoulders, our fates entwined with it.

CHAPTER 44

RED

The plan was mercifully simple. Aside from the front entrance where prisoners were processed, the rest of the entrances were mostly unguarded, relying on magic to keep unwanted visitors out and prisoners inside. Anyone with godlike powers who attempted to enter would trip the alarms and cause a lockdown, while any human who was foolish enough to pass through the entrances would be vaporized by the magical power vibrating through the facility.

I lived at the intersection of both: more powerful than a human and less so than a god and made of pure magic like the barriers themselves. Theoretically then, I could walk through with ease. Rama and iNyanga seemed confident in that assessment, and since they helped build the prison, I relied on them to know what they were talking about. We could only hope that the security measures hadn't been improved in the past thousand generations. The gods were not known for their ability, or desire, to adapt to new ways of doing things, so it felt like as good a plan as any.

"Be careful," Rose said, squeezing me tightly one last

time. There was an unspoken understanding that this would probably be the last time we spoke to each other, but neither of us said that. After all, we both should have died a dozen times, and yet, we were still standing. Perhaps we could pull off another miracle.

As I walked away from her, stomach tightening in pain and loss, Rama's voice echoed through my head. "Can you hear me?"

"Yes," I replied, confirming the connection we established a few hours earlier. Hepit and Aditi were busy helping Rose and Hypnos, leaving Rama to guide me through the prison. "I don't like this."

"Don't worry, sweetheart," Rama cooed. "I was already in your head. Now, we've just made it official."

"You had better not be looking through my memories and thoughts," I growled. "Those are private."

"The only thing I would be interested in your pretty little head would be what you thought of me, and you told me all that last night, so your memories and thoughts are safe."

I tried to hide my distaste for his words as I exited the bar and made my way through the city. The worst part of it all, of everything, was that he wasn't wrong. I hated myself, especially my duplicitous body, for being attracted to someone so cavalier—a god, nonetheless. But even if my rational mind could push him away, there was clearly something about him that my body craved, almost animal-istically.

It didn't matter. Once this was over, he would give me the location of the portal to the Dark Planet, and he would be gone from my life, or I would be dead before then.

"Turn left here," Rama said in my ear.

I did as he said and made my way down a dark alley

that broke into a large field, on the other side of which was the Crystal Keep, glittering a hundred different colors against the stars. Rose would continue towards the front of the Crystal Keep with Hypnos and demand to see her beloved, while I slid through a service entrance in the back, barely used save for emergencies.

I kept my head on a swivel on my way across the field. iNyanga was right when she said nobody would be watching the back of the facility. "Nobody is dumb enough to break in without a purpose, except you, of course," she'd told me, and that made me feel not even a little bit better.

Though the Crystal Keep was built to house gods, it was mostly filled with dissidents from around the galaxy. They couldn't enter the Celestial Realm without a god, and no gods cared enough about the denizens of the universe to risk themselves for a mere mortal.

"You should be nearing the entrance," Rama whispered.

Sure enough, I had just come across a dirt path that circled the Crystal Keep. The prison stood one hundred feet tall, made of knobby crystals that undulated together to form one seamless structure, save for a small slit at its base big enough for a god to walk through.

"I see it." My voice trembled as I spoke. "Are you sure this will work?"

"Eighty percent. Maybe ninety."

"That's not nearly high enough for my liking."

"It's pretty good, given that you're about to breach the highest security facility in the universe."

I grit my teeth. "Fair enough."

There was no point drawing out the inevitable. Either I would be captured, vaporized, or remain intact the moment I walked through the beam, and the suspense was as bad as the act. I closed my eyes and started walking. The beam resisted me, but my body held fast against its incredible power. If anything, the beam was making me stronger.

"You're almost there," Rama said. "Keep moving!"

I fought my way through until I finally tumbled through to the other side, coming to a stop against the far wall. I breathed heavily as the strange energy pulsed through me, at the same time foreign and familiar.

"I'm through," I said, standing up.

"Wonderful," Rama said. "You are just as spectacular as I imagined."

"Save the compliments for when I get out of this alive." I peered the corridor. "Now, where am I going?"

"Relax, Gabrielle. This is the easy part."

"Famous last words."

"Then you do not deny that you made this abomination?" Zeus's voice boomed from the dais. We had been at it for hours, talking in circles as the six members of the Board peppered us with the same questions over and over again.

"Hey!" I shouted. "I thought I told you I don't like being called that!"

"Once again," one of Brahma's heads shouted, "we do not care about the feelings of a mortal, especially one that has been turned into an *abomination* such as yourself."

"Ukko," Tengri said. "It's your turn once again. Do you have any questions for the defendant?"

They had made it very clear that I was not on trial. I was nothing but evidence of Nox's shame, her betrayal of the Board, the pantheon, and the universe. It was humiliating and demeaning to be reduced to nothing but an object. I wished it was the first time I felt like it but growing up in America as a Black woman and a monster to boot, it was an all-too-common sensation.

Ukko shifted some papers around and squinted. "Your actions in the Fairy Realm went against the spirit and letter of the law as it is written. On top of that, you were expressly forbidden by this council from interfering with that matter, and yet, you presented your champion with the Xirgolov and instructions on how to charge it. Explain to me how this alone is not enough to find you guilty on all charges?"

"I have nothi—" Nox began, before the doors to the chamber opened wide, letting in the first slashes of light, aside from the dais, that we had seen in hours.

"What is the meaning of this?" Svarog slammed his hands on the table.

The thumping of thick boots was overpowered by Athena's strong voice. "I'm sorry, your honors, but there has been a complication."

"Preposterous!" Osiris shouted. "This is a closed chamber where we work to decide the fate of a god. Nothing is more important than it, and nothing may interfere with it."

Athena bowed her head. "I'm sorry, your majesties, but it appears Nox's child has appeared, along with the paramour of this gorgon thing."

Rose? Here? Panic washed away my smile when I realized what this meant. They had plenty of ire directed at Rose, and she walked in and handed herself to them on a silver platter.

"Rose?" Zeus said. "Rose Briar? Champion of the Dream Realm, uniter of the Underworld, and the prophet that raised the Sunken Kingdom?"

Athena glanced down at her notes. "It doesn't say all that, but if she is the one engaged to this one, then yes."

Engaged? That meant Rose found my ring, the one I left on the table in our apartment when Athena kidnapped me, and she said yes. *She said yes.* My heart backflipped while I tried to keep a solemn face.

"If this is true," Tengri said, leaning forward, "then she is as culpable as Nox and could be a powerful character witness against her."

Svarog rustled through some papers. "It says here she was gifted two blessings, one by Hypnos and the other by Persephone—a direct violation of our charter—making her quite powerful, especially for a mortal."

"Should I have her arrested?" Athena asked, still standing at attention.

Zeus shook his head. "Let this play out. She is here to advocate for the accused, and we will let her, as per our customs. She will dig Nox's grave, and then once she has had her day in court, we will take care of her. Any objections?" Zeus looked at the other gods. No hands went up. "Make it noted in the minutes that this motion carries." He turned back to Athena. "Take them away."

The bar demagnetized, and I was able to move again. Nox rose without another word, but I wouldn't be so polite. As Athena walked towards me, I tried to push her away to no avail. She slapped me across the face, sending me to the ground. I reached out with my hands to use my power, and a surge of electricity flowed through me. Despite the pain, I latched onto my jailer. The electricity carried from me to her, and our shrieks echoed through the chamber.

"ENOUGH!" Ukko's voice boomed. He snapped his fingers and the electricity stopped. Athena and I both fell to the ground, our bodies smelling of charred flesh. "This is unbecoming of a prisoner and of a soldier. Pull yourself together, Athena! I expect more from a representative of this court!"

"Yes, sir. I'm sorry, sir. It won't happen again." Athena pulled me to my feet. She had recovered quickly, but I was still sluggish in my movements.

"See that it doesn't," Brahma said. "Otherwise, we will find somebody else who can carry out our orders without such unseemly conduct."

"Yes, sir." For the first time Athena sounded contrite, scared even, and I knew then that she could feel fear. If she did anything to hurt Rose, I would make sure that I was the cause of her fear.

Oh, Rose.

I knew she would come.

But I wished that for once she would have stayed home and left me to my fate. Whatever I'd gotten myself into was too big for me, and for her. There wasn't any getting out of this one, unless she had a miracle up her sleeve. Then again, knowing Rose, she might. Even if we somehow made it out of this, though, where would we hide, when the Board controlled the entire universe?

CHAPTER 46
NIMUE

It might have been made with the intent to scare and unnerve people, but King Hastur's palace was exactly my aesthetic. High gothic ceilings with twisted sculptures lining the walls, three-story portraits of monsters fighting humanity for dominance of the universe—and winning— elaborate chandeliers made of bone and sinewy dripping wax along the floor, dark black embroidered plush rugs. It would have been perfect if not for all the people, but such was royal life. Unlimited power in exchange for tedious duty to the realm.

Cassandra snaked me through the partygoers milling around, chatting with each other, acting as if they weren't hideous and wondrous at the same time, as if a sentient blob of green slime was as normal as the sun rising in the east and setting in the west.

The hallway broke into an elaborate ballroom filled with still more oddities. A twenty-piece orchestra played, and the monsters waltzed with each other, as royals had a thousand times in the halls of my palace. Around the floor, partygoers drank from the skulls of unspeakable horrors with three eye holes and long mouths.

On the ornate onyx staircase at the far end of the room stood four women, regal, above the fray. The first wore a black crown of bone, with the forest cracked upon her face, revealing the green glow of the trees and the heart of the forest. Next to her, a bald woman with the universe spinning around where her head should be. The stars dripped down to her shoulders, where her dark skin took over and continued into a pluming white dress. Her red eyes glowed as she stared out into oblivion.

On the other side of her perched a woman with alabaster skin, eyes, and hair, with six horns protruding from around her head. Her mouth was wider than it had any reason to be, with a hundred sharp black teeth showing whenever she smiled. Finally, at the other end of the stairwell, a woman with black holes where her eyes should be, holes that cracked across her face, and another for her mouth, wore a black thorn crown and spoke with an older, flayed woman whose face was torn into a hundred pieces. She wore a blood-red gown made of meat.

"Those are the princesses whom Hastur has chosen for his harem and personal guard," Cassandra whispered. "Some call them the lucky ones, but I know the truth; the only true luck for them would be a swift death."

The one with the horns waved when she saw us and called us over to her. Cassandra pulled me close and spun me across the dance floor to the light tune of the music.

"Cassandra," the demon princess said, her voice raspy. "You escaped this place, and yet you return every year to mock us."

"That is not my intention, Elvira," Cassandra said with a bow. "I only wish to pay my respects to you, my sisters."

"We are not sisters," said the girl with the forest hidden inside her face. She blinked, trying to hide the hatred in her eyes. "You have fallen out of favor with the dark king."

"I'm sorry, Delilah." Cassandra, who had been so confident, shrunk like a wilting violet. "If I knew I would lose you all, I never would have left."

"And yet you did, and now you have returned to flaunt it. Is this the new princess you brought to curry favor with the king?" The girl with black holes for eyes broke her conversation with the flayed woman and eyed me up and down. "So that he might bestow his grace on you yet again?"

"That's not—" Cassandra started, then looked down and gulped. "Yes, this is her, Bethel. Nimue they call her."

I held out my hand, but they all looked at me coldly. The final princess, the bald one with the universe dripping to her shoulders, sneered. "He's going to hate you. You're already twisted. He likes to make his princesses in his image."

"Is that how you became like that?" I asked.

"Like what?" she snapped. "Better than I ever was before Hastur found me?"

"She didn't mean anything by it, Lydia." Cassandra stepped between us. "I promise, she's really very sweet."

"I should hope not," Delilah said. "Sweet is the last thing he wants."

"Yeah," Elvira added. "He eats sweet for breakfast."

"Not true, sister," Bethel said, studying me more closely. "He throws it in the trash."

I felt cornered, unsure which direction to take the conversation, when all the lights crackled off at once and a yellow light appeared at the top of the stairs. Only when it descended the stairs did I realize the light came from the cape wrapped around the King in Yellow's body, and that Hastur was making a beeline right for me, his two glowing eyes tracking me from under his cloak.

CHAPTER 47

RED

Rama lied. Navigating through the Crystal Keep was not the easy part. The corridors weaved circuitously, splintering in every direction, making it difficult for even somebody who helped design the Crystal Keep to follow.

"Turn right," Rama said in my ear.

I poked my head around the corner to make sure I wasn't about to walk into a trap. At least he was right about there not being a lot of guards inside the facility. If I had to walk these halls while worrying about a thousand soldiers, I would have already been caught, no doubt about it.

I turned as instructed and took off down the shimmering hallway. The walls glowed like somebody shone a light through a prism, the flat light absorbing all shadows and preventing me with any good place to hide.

"The door to the left," Rama said. "Go inside."

I found the white metal door and stepped into the room. "We've been wandering around these halls for half an hour. Pretty soon our diversion will be too late."

"I'm working on it, okay? They seem to have divided the corridors even more than in my initial designs to accommodate more cell blocks. The disadvantage of jailing dissidents is that you need a place to house them."

"I'm not looking for a lesson in architecture. Get me to those controls before this has all been for nothing."

"We're getting close, just—"

I heard footsteps on the other side of the door and froze. "Shut up."

"Excuse me?" Rama said.

I didn't answer. I was busy looking around the room for a place to hide. Luckily, even a state-of-the-art facility to house gods and monsters needed supplies, and I stumbled into a janitor's closet. I rolled behind a bucket, placing several buckets of industrial cleaner in front of me.

I hadn't gotten settled before the door opened and a grumpy-looking crystal golem clomped inside. Their body didn't glow like the prison walls, but it still had the same colorful fractal pattern.

"What's happening?" Rama whispered.

"Shhhh."

The golem's eyes flashed, and they swiveled their head in my direction, staring for a long moment, but then thought better of it and pulled a bucket out of the room, grumbling and grunting as it clinked down the hallway. When it was gone, I rolled myself out of my hiding spot and brushed myself off.

"Why didn't you tell me this place was maintained by crystal golems?" I hissed.

"Did you think the gods would deign to lower themselves down to clean toilets and mop floors? No, we reserve ourselves for the more dignified parts of running a universe."

"And you wonder why everyone hates you."

"No, I don't. And no, they don't." I could feel Rama's

smile, and my lip turned up in disgust. "I have a bead on your location, and the control room. We're almost there, just two more corridors. Hurry up."

I rushed out of the room, even more worried than I'd been before. I was prepared to fight a god, or their minions, as long as they were made of flesh, but I had never fought sentient rocks before. I didn't know if my daggers would be enough to do the trick. The hallway snaked left and right until it dead-ended at another doorway. I pulled the daggers out of my belt and took a deep breath. The doors opened for me, and I slipped inside.

A large glass window looked down on a thousand cells that seemed to extend into the heavens higher than the Crystal Keep should allow. In front of the window spanned a long console, carved from the same crystal as the walls, with hundreds of levers and buttons on it. Two crystal golems sat at the controls, and when I walked into the room they turned and roared.

"I thought you said this place was unguarded!" I shouted at Rama.

"I said it was mostly unguarded!" he shouted back. "This room used to be controlled autonomously."

I stabbed my dagger towards one of the golem's heads, but it just bounced off and stung my hands. "How do I kill them?"

"The back of their throats is their weak spot. Hit them there and they should explode."

I spun to the other golem just as it went to push a button calling for help. I kicked it away and it slammed into the wall. The other golem grabbed me around the arms as the first one leapt off the wall and back towards me. I vaulted over the golem holding me, and the two of them crashed into each other. As they rose, I stuck my daggers into their throats, and they exploded into a million pieces around the room, embedding into the walls, floor, and console.

I paused for a breath then said, "Now, how do I open these cells and disarm the restraints?"

Rama led me through a series of buttons and levers, until a section of the crystal console parted, and a big red button rose from it. "That is the emergency failsafe. If you push that button, everything goes to hell."

"Now you're speaking my language." I said. "Tell me when."

"Soon," Rama said. "They're almost in position."

CHAPTER 48
ARIEL

My mother did not birth me, but she did love me and raise me after I came to the Dream Realm. Before then, I was an orphan, on my own until I could no longer stomach it. I didn't know true love until I drifted into the Dream Realm during a bout of consumption, and my mother found me wandering the bogs. Back then, I didn't know much about her, except that she was one of Loki's attendants. I was young, and she took pity on me. She begged for leave from her duties and traveled with me across the world, through the Dark Domain, into the Land of Oz, until we finally reached the Obsidian Spindle. We made the best time we could, but by the time we arrived there was nothing we could do. My body was dead, and I was stuck in the Dream Realm.

My mother agreed to raise me and teach me everything she knew. It was this kind heart that Hypnos fell in love with, and what made him consider her for his blessing.

But that was a long way off then.

In those first days, when it was just her and I—they were the first days of my whole life I was happy, and I cherished them. She was not my mother, but she was the only mother I would ever know, who truly looked out for my best interests. A mother who wanted the best for me. She wanted to protect me because she loved me, not because I hid some secret. There was nothing in it for her, but she treated me well anyway.

On our way back to the bogs, she brought me to a field filled with the most beautiful flowers I had ever seen. Orchids, she called them, mixed with Calla lilies, and each had exactly six sides. Godflowers, she explained. They grew on only one place in Urgu, on the grave of Hypnos's one and only love, Pasithea.

Seeing a dried version on the monk's book told me all I needed to know about where to go next. It was subtle enough that nobody who found it would have given it a second thought, but precise enough that I knew where to go.

The meadow was just as I remembered it, full of love, life, and light. I thanked the driver Queen Aine appointed for me and asked him to wait for me, then walked slowly through the fields of the brilliant pink flowers. My touch sent little beads of light exploding into the air in a brilliant display. It had been my mother's favorite place in the world, and on our visit that day, she told me she loved me for the first time.

I took a deep breath, watching the lights flutter about, and I felt my brain crack open like it had been ripped in half. I screamed out, gripping my head and writhing about the wonderful flowers that had until then given me nothing but joy.

After a few seconds it was over, and I sank to the ground, panting. My eyes fluttered open as I tried to come to terms with the new memories shooting through my brain. Something was still blocking me from accessing them all, but thoughts of my mother and memories of us together shot through my brain. I smiled brightly, newly remembering.

As the memories passed by, whizzing through my mind, another memory grew into a giant and slammed into my eyes until it was all I could see: a chapel, in the middle of a field, overlooking the Emerald City.

That was where I had to go next, and where I would find the eye.

CHAPTER 49
ROSE

My stomach fell into my knees as a pair of crystal golems led us through the Keep into a small room filled with several long tables. It wasn't unlike the prison meeting rooms that I'd seen on television, but these were made of the same crystal and seemed to rise as an extension of a Keep itself.

"You should sit," Hypnos said as he slid onto one of the benches. "They might be a while."

"Are you kidding?" I said, pacing. "I'm way too nervous for that."

"Well, you're making me nervous."

"That's a good instinct." I nodded my head. "There are just so many reasons to be nervous right now."

He pulled off his sunglasses and handed them to me, rubbing his eyes. "Can you hold these a minute?"

I grabbed the glasses and stuffed them into the pockets of my dress before smoothing the wrinkles out of it the best I could. Then, I pulled out the tracking device and switched it on. Chelle's dot was nearly on top of us now. Any moment, she would walk through the door, and we would be united once again. After that, there was the matter of escaping. I had tried to count the turns, but there were so many that I lost track. I hoped that Hepit could do the impossible and lead us out of the prison as she promised.

I wore grooves on the crystal floor with my footsteps for several more minutes until the door finally opened and Nox shuffled into the room, wearing bracelets on her arms and legs that glowed a brilliant blue.

"Those are restraining bracers," Hepit said in my ear. "Once Red opens the doors to the prison, they'll fall away. That's when you have to run for the front."

Nox gazed down at the floor as she plodded forward. She had lost a lot of weight. Behind her came Chelle, and my heart shot right back into my chest. I had been told not to touch the prisoners, but I leapt over the table and wrapped her in a hug so tightly that I worried it hurt her.

"Chelle!" I shouted, burying my face in her neck. "You smell like home."

"And you feel like home," Chelle replied, her restraining bracers resting on the small of my back. "I missed you."

"Oh look, Chelle," Nox said. "It's the Dreamer and the cad."

"Which one am I?" Hypnos said.

"It doesn't matter," Nox snapped. "As always, you're a day late and a dollar short."

"I'm happy to see you, too," he said.

"I'm glad to see you too, in a way," she replied. "But you're an idiot for coming here."

"She's right," Chelle added, kissing me on the forehead. "This is super dangerous. What are you doing here?"

The guards forcefully separated us then guided Nox and Chelle to the other side of the table.

"What do you mean 'what are you doing here'? This is

kind of our thing. You get kidnapped, and I come to find you."

"Hey," she chuckled. "That first time it was me who came for you."

"And now you're the damsel. Being on this side of things is more fun."

Chelle smiled, before her eye dropped to the ring on my finger. "I see you found it."

"I did." I spun the ring. "I hope you don't mind. It was too beautiful to sit in that stuffy old box."

She shook her head. "No. I'm just upset I didn't get that proposal."

"You can do it now," I whispered. "If it will make you better."

"We're in prison," Nox growled. "It's not very romantic here."

"All the more reason," ignoring Nox's glare, keeping my attention on Chelle. "Who knows if you'll ever get out of here, or if we'll ever have the chance again?"

"And you'll still want to be with me, even if I never do?"

She didn't know we were there to break her out, and I couldn't let it slip, so I just played along, trying to find ways to extend the conversation until Red was in place. "Always."

Her eyes filled with tears, and it took her a moment to choke them back. "Give me the ring," she said. I placed it on her palm, and she clasped her hand around it. She took a long, shuddering breath, then raised her head to meet my eyes. "Rose Briar. Will you marry me?"

Even though I knew it was coming, even though we were already engaged as far as I was concerned, her question took me aback, and now tears flowed down my face, too. "Yes, yes, I will. Of course I will."

She placed the ring on my finger and collapsed into my lap. "I love you so much."

"I love you too." I leaned down to whisper into her ear. "And I'll always come for you."

"How touching," Nox groaned. "If only you could get us out of here."

"NOW!" Hepir shouted.

"Funny story…" I started as red lights shot through every surface as the cuffs on Chelle's arms and legs fell free. "That's exactly what we're here to do."

CHAPTER 50
CHELLE

"What did you—" I gaped at my restraining bracelets on the floor. "Did you do this?"

"Of course I did." Rose grinned and took my hand. "Now we have to go, quickly."

Two crystal golems materialized, but Nox threw several shadow bolts at them, and they exploded instantly.

"And here I didn't think you had it in you," Nox said to Hypnos. "Perhaps I underestimated you."

"We'll talk about it later!" Hypnos screamed, flinging open the door.

"This was really stupid, Rose!" I screamed as my feet pounded against the floor. "Now you're going to be hunted like me."

"When will you learn?" Rose turned to me as another pair of golems and other guards headed towards us. "The world isn't worth living in without you. I will not let you rot in prison alone, even if that means I have to rot in prison with you."

She clasped her hands together, and a thunderous wave crackled through the room and snapped the crystal golems in half. Hypnos put another to sleep, and Nox finished off the rest with some shadow flames. I couldn't believe that I was the weakest of the group.

"Come on!" Rose shouted, pulling me down a hallway. How she knew where to go, I didn't know, but I hoped that however she was getting her directions, she was right. "Over here!"

We spun around a corner and the room molded around us, blocking off all the exits and revealing another room with a dozen crystal golems and even more soldiers. Leading them was Athena, clad in battle armor.

"Did you really think you could escape?" she snarled. "Stupid."

I pressed my hands out. *"Fulmen ignem!"* My fire bolt crashed into her crest, sending her flying backwards. It felt good to smash her a little bit.

"You and Rose take the golems," Nox said. "Hypnos, subdue the soldiers. I'll take Athena."

"No, Mom!" Hypnos said. "She's too powerful."

"Please," the god of darkness said with a chuckle. "She's nothing compared to me."

Nox disappeared then reappeared in front of Athena. She raised her hands into the air and darkness descended on the room. Dozens of shadow creatures rose up to join in the battle, and she leveled attack after attack at Athena.

"Be careful," Rose said to me. Her powerful burst of lightning through the air cut down three golems.

"That's funny," I said. "Given the circumstances."

I turned to a group of four. *"Acidum spiritus!"* Hideous green slime shot from my mouth and landed on the golems. Wherever it touched, the golems melted, leaving puddles of ooze on the ground.

Hypnos cast a spell and the remaining soldiers fell to the ground. A door appeared.

"Exit!" Rose shouted. "We can—"

As she spoke, a lightning bolt cracked in the middle of the room. In the scorched crystal, a figure rose, bearded and holding a lightning bolt. It was Zeus, grown to the size of the room.

"Enough!" He tossed a lightning bolt towards Nox, electrocuting her. She fell to the ground. "We have tried to be fair, but now I see that it is impossible with the likes of you." He walked over Nox's fried body and hoisted it upwards. "By order of the Board, I sentence you to a life of servitude, to amend for the many generations you have fought against us."

He reached his fist into Nox's chest and when he pulled it out, a ghostly blue apparition flailed against him. He stuffed her into a box of light and sealed it shut.

"Mom!" Hypnos shouted. "Go! I'll hold him back."

"But we—" I started, but it was no use. He was in a rage. Hypnos slammed Zeus into a wall, knocking his mother free. As I watched them fight, I saw Nox's body rise from the ground, her eyes now a pale white, with no life behind them.

"Get those two!" Zeus shouted to Nox. "I'll handle this one."

Nox nodded, and again, the lights left the room. It didn't bother Nox one bit, being the goddess of darkness, and she moved toward us with menace. She formed a tentacle out of inky blackness and whipped it at me.

"What are you doing, Nox?" I shouted.

"She can't hear you," Rose said, pressing her finger to her ear. "We have to get out of there now."

"I can't abandon her," I said. "That's not—"

"Trust me." Rose's tone was stern. "She's already gone, and you will be too if you don't leave now."

Nox flung another tentacle in our direction, and I pulled Rose down to avoid the blow.

A dozen shadow creatures materialized as we fought back the attack. Rose squeezed my hand tight and bolted for the door, dragging me along with her. "Let's go!"

"Fine, but I don't like it."

"That's fine with me," Rose said.

"*Lux!*" I screamed as we passed into the hall beyond, sending a massive explosion of light through the room and dispelling the shadows, at least for a moment.

We couldn't outrun our captors forever. Even if we escaped this prison, they would never stop until Zeus and the Board had us back under their control. They were insatiable, and they hated dissidents, especially ones that made them look foolish.

CHAPTER 51

NIMUE

A shiver went down my spine, but also a rush of exhilaration, looking at King Hastur. He had power; pure, uncut power. It oozed out of his every pore, and he knew it. The four princesses parted to let him pass. They tracked him with a combination of hatred and utter fascination, as did everyone in his orbit, but his eyes were on me.

The music cut from the dance floor into a haunting, slow ballad when Hastur raised his arm to wave to his loyal subjects. No matter how evil the person, nobody could rule through fear alone. Fear was a powerful motivator, but I saw admiration in every face in the crowd. Yes, the King in Yellow might be a bad man, he might be pure evil, but he controlled the crowd, and they loved him for it.

"My loyal servants." His voice was smooth and slick like black ice as the words rolled off his tongue. He held no fear of these people, even the conniving ones that worked to destroy him. Any good ruler knew that there would always be a subsection of people working to undermine them, and while it was good to snuff them out, sometimes it was better to keep their plans going, let them ferret each other out, so that you could destroy them with one fatal blow.

"Welcome to my Hellonic Ball." His eyes hadn't left mine the whole time he moved forward. "Old acquaintances and new friends gather together on this night to celebrate...me, and my rule. I have bestowed on you the greatest gifts on this dark planet, and tonight, we indulge in them all to remind ourselves that this world is ours for the taking."

An applause started small and then crescendoed into a roar. Hastur knew how to control a room, and how to fete those that worked for him. No ruler, regardless of their power, could rule a planet by themselves. They needed sycophants to carry out their will; to infiltrate every corner of the planet and carry out their will. It was often laughable how cheap it was to buy people off and bring them around to your way of thinking. Laud them, keep them fat and happy, and they will bow to you. Even if the thought of it makes them queasy, and they will allow your power to grow until it consumes them. Every horrible face in this ball was consumed completely by the King in Yellow.

"Now," Hastur said with a flourish as he continued down the stairs. "Eat, drink, and be merry, my friends, for tomorrow is not promised, and yesterday is over. All we have is tonight!"

With that, he flicked his wrists and fireworks popped off in his hands and exploded all around the room. There was another round of applause.

"My princesses," Hastur purred as they gathered around him. He kissed their hands as they fawned over him, weak as putty in his hands. As he gave them all a bit of attention, his eyes still tracked to me. "And my wayward love, Cassandra. It's always so lovely to see you." The darkness under his cloak became a vicious smile. "And what have you brought me tonight?"

"This is Nimue, my lord," Cassandra said. "I found her on the islands of fire, the last living descendant of King Ithsan."

The King in Yellow tsked. "A horrible bore, that one. I thought we destroyed his seed and salted the Earth so they should never return."

"I thought the same, and yet, here she is."

Hastur waved the princesses away and came face to face with me. "I must say, you are quite fetching. It's almost as if somebody designed you to be appealing to me."

His glowing eyes narrowed, and he gave a knowing smile. I swallowed loudly, wondering if he knew I was a fraud, but there was nothing to do now. Two hundred or more of his feckless royal family stood between me and the room, not to mention guards, and his power to flay me before I could run ten feet from him.

"I appreciate that," I replied coolly. "That is quite an honor, coming from you."

He circled me and I lost my breath, as if it were stolen from me. "It is an honor. Your father was weak and fell quickly. Tell me, would you like a seat at my table, so that you can feel what real power tastes like?"

I nodded meekly. Powerful men detested powerful women, so I did everything to appear less than I was to him. "It would be a great honor. I have lived in squalor for so long, and this place is so grand. I would so much love to see more of it." My eyes left his eyes and found the nose necklace he wore around his neck. It was white as ivory, and strung through the nostrils, so it hung upside down.

He held out his hand. "Then come."

This was it. My moment. I reached past his hand to

touch the nose, and then ran my hand up his arm to find the gap between his glove and his braces, at the wrist. However, when I felt for it, I found nothing but a bit of thick, black cloth.

"A pity," Hastur growled. "I thought perhaps you could see past the lies Rapunzel told you."

He snapped his fingers, and it was as if I was ripped apart from the inside and turned inside out, my organs shifting and binding together. I couldn't scream. When it was over, every breath was filled with agony. My eyes teared and filled with water, but I saw Cassandra, wearing my skin, turn and smile at the King in Yellow.

"Then I have done well, my lord?"

He kissed her lightly. "Very well, my love. Welcome back to my graces."

She had betrayed me.

CHAPTER 52
ROSE

"Left!" Hepit screamed into my ear. "No, right!"

The passages of the prison were changing faster than we could keep up, with every turn seeming to take us deeper into the circuitous maze of the Crystal Keep and further from the entrance.

"*Fractus!*" I shouted, pressing my hand against the wall. It slammed down and shattered. Behind it, the hallway split into four directions. "Where now?"

"Second from the right, and hurry. I feel Nox's magic close."

"How did you know what was happening with Nox?" I asked as I followed Hepit's directions.

"This isn't the first time Zeus has used mind control to avoid fighting his own battles. Unfortunately, it's kind of his M-O, and we're not out of the woods yet."

Sure enough, she no sooner said those words than four black shadows appeared, weapons swinging wildly.

"*Lux!*" Chelle said, and her sunbeam cut through them with little effort.

"Nice shot, babe!" I shouted as I grabbed her hand and headed in the direction that Hepit had told us to.

"We're never going to make it out of here," Chelle said, holding the stitch in her side. "This is impossible."

We stopped to catch our breath at another intersection, waiting for Hepit's orders.

"Nothing is impossible," I said to Chelle. "If the last year has taught me anything, it's that."

"I'm not sure I've learned anything in the past year. It feels like just a bunch of stuff that's happened to us."

"And we survived it." I kissed her. "We'll survive this, too."

"How cute." All the light drained from the room as the god of darkness materialized. Her voice was dull and monotonous. "You cannot escape, foolish one."

"*Fractus!*" I screamed, breaking through the wall between us and the next hallway, as we sped away from her. We weren't twenty feet down the next hallway before the darkness latched onto our legs and pulled us back, like tentacles from an enormous sea monster. "Let go of us!"

"*Lux!*" Chelle shouted again, but before her light could even materialize, Nox covered her hands with uncompromising shadow, and the sunbeams dissipated in her hands.

"In another life, perhaps you might have made good pets." Her eyes were white and lifeless.

Her tentacles whipped at us with deadly precision. She was fast, but I was determined. *This isn't how it ends for us.* Our story wasn't over yet. There had to be something that I could do to combat her incredible power. Perhaps if I couldn't control the light around her, I could control the darkness instead.

"Oh, great darkness." *That was how Nimue started, right?* "I beseech you to help me. Nox, your goddess, has been lost to her enemies, and she needs our help to save her. Please, help free us, so that we may escape and save her."

Nox held me upside down and laughed into my face. "That was a good try, but there is no calling for help this time." Sure enough, the darkness did not come for me. Instead, it squeezed me even tighter, until it was so tight around my chest that the breath left my lungs. My cheeks flushed as I gasped for air, and the room blurred.

"No!" Chelle screamed. "Let us go!"

I couldn't see anything but the orange glow from Chelle's eyes when she spoke. Such a thing would not have worked on Nox if she had her faculties about her, but somehow, miraculously, the tentacles unlatched from my body, and I fell to the ground.

I looked up at Nox. Her eyes were completely orange, and she stood at attention. "What did you do?"

Chelle waved her hand in front of Nox's face, but the goddess didn't move. "I think I might have overwritten Zeus's command. I didn't know I could do that."

"Whoa," I replied. "Can you get her to do other stuff?"

"Um," Chelle scratched her head and then looked up at Nox, both of their eyes glowed orange. "Stand on one foot." Without a word, Nox raised her right leg. "Clap your hands." Sure enough, she did as she was told, looking off into the distance. "This is awesome."

"Awesome, maybe, but can she do anything useful, like get us out of here?"

"Let's see." Chelle's eyes glowed orange. "Nox, get us out of this prison, to safety."

Nox nodded and the tentacles reached towards us again. I couldn't explain it, except to say that I knew they were no longer there to hurt me. They were gentle. They coiled around me until I was completely consumed with darkness.

I watched in a haze as we bounced between the corridors, through crystal golems, and down a different series of hallways and pipes. Finally, the Crystal Keep finally spat us out of a side entrance.

"We did it," I said, breathing heavy. "We made it out."

Chelle looked up at Nox, whose eyes still glowed orange. "Yeah, but I think we left Nox's soul in there."

"We have her body. That's something." I looked up at the goddess. "Besides, no offense, but I don't really care about her. I care about you, and as far as I'm concerned, you're safe, and that's what matters."

Chelle chuckled. "Oh honey, we are so far from safe. This may have been the easiest part."

I grabbed her hand. "Come on. Let me introduce you to some people who might be able to help us."

Chelle pointed to Nox. "What do we do with her?"

"Bring her along. I have a feeling she'll be useful."

"Right," Chelle said. Her eyes turned orange. "Come along, Nox."

CHAPTER 53
RED

It was a thing of chaotic beauty. I pressed the button and every cell on the block opened. Hundreds, thousands of inmates bolted from their cells, their restraints falling away. They overwhelmed the guards, the golems, and everyone as they swarmed the hallways seeking freedom, confrontation, or both. I heard their shouts grow louder until their footsteps rushed past the door like a stampede.

"Time to go," Rama said in my ear. "Lose yourself in the chaos but follow my directions to the exit."

The door slid open upon my approach, revealing dozens of different species and races sprinting past the door. I waited for a break in the action and joined the crowd. As we made it through the hallways, the crowd broke into different groups, each following a different set of corridors towards what they believed to be freedom.

I followed Rama's directions left and right down the crowded corridors. Then, as I turned a corner, I heard an explosion, and the bodies of a dozen prisoners flew back , mangled and bloodied. I peered around the corridor to see several soldiers holding their arms out in a magic stance.

The other prisoners reached for chunks of broken crystal and ran towards their attackers once again. I joined them, and as the soldiers were distracted by the onslaught, I pulled out my daggers and stabbed two of them through the stomach. With a break in the formation, the rest of the prisoners filled the gap and overwhelmed the others without much effort.

With the guards swallowed up, we continued down the hallway. It felt like a victory parade, almost with the levity and excitement that crackled through us all. When we reached the next break, ten crystal golems waited for us.

"Go for their necks!" I shouted, and they did. A few lost limbs in the action, but they quickly took down the crystal golem horde.

"Rama," I said, panting. "How much further?"

There was silence for a moment, then he sighed into my ear. "I'm sorry, Gabrielle, but there's been a problem."

"Are Chelle and Rose okay?" I asked.

"For now, but Nox's soul has been taken by Zeus, and we can't defeat the Board without her."

"But Chelle and Rose are okay?" I asked, more forcefully than the last time.

"As far as I know, yes," Rama said. "But you don—"

I stabbed my dagger through one of the final golems and it exploded around me. "Then I don't care."

"Your friends can't survive without our help. The Board will chase them across the universe. We can protect them, or we can...not."

I rushed down the hallway weaving through the crowd. "Are you threatening me?"

"No, I'm negotiating with you," Rama said. "Your friends need our protection, and we need Nox's soul."

"And how am I supposed to find that, huh?" I asked, as I swerved to the right.

"Easy, you get captured again. They will bring you to Zeus, and you will impress on him that you are the catalyst."

"The catalyst?" I asked. "What's that supposed to mean?"

"When Nox designed her plan, she needed three beings of pure magic to use as catalysts to use to create her new world order."

"Pure magic?" It clicked then. "You are talking about Chelle and me, aren't you?"

"Yes," Rama replied. "That is what it means to be a key, and why you are so feared by the Board."

"And you knew about this?" I said.

"I knew what you were, but not how she meant to use you. Nobody does but Nox, which is why you need to get her back."

"And what's to stop Zeus from just killing me?"

"Morbid curiosity and hubris. You are, at your core, a human, and he thinks quite lowly of your kind."

"You're taking a mighty chance with my life," I said, turning another corner.

"You do this for us, and we'll protect your friends, whether you succeed or not. You have my word."

"I really and truly hate you," I said.

"I'll be with you the whole time."

"That's not very comforting, since you're walking me straight into impending doom," I snapped back.

We reached another large room, this time filled with hundreds of soldiers and golems, while our numbers had dwindled. They had taken many of us into custody again, and things were looking bleak for the prisoners.

I knew what I had to do, but I didn't like it. It was giving my life up and putting it in the hands of a god. The important thing was that Rose and Chelle would be safe if I helped Rama. I would give up my life any day for them, so really this was a no brainer.

"Who is the third catalyst?" I asked.

"We don't know yet," Rama replied. "Which is another reason we need Nox."

The soldiers advanced on our little party. There were ten of us against a hundred of them, and we all knew the score. I wasn't the first one to drop my weapons, which was something, and I was doing it for a noble cause, which was something else, but I didn't like any part of giving up.

"I surrender," I said, dropping to my knees and falling to the ground, prone.

A soldier tied my hands together behind me, the restraints uncomfortably tight. When I was helpless, they kicked away my weapons, and then gave me a kick to my face, knocking me backward into a pile of my comrades.

Now, we were truly in this together.

CHAPTER 54

ARIEL

The Church of the Six hadn't always been the dominant religion in Urgu. In his younger days Hypnos insisted that there be no religion in the Dream Realm. He certainly didn't want to laud and idolize the gods that he was responsible for imprisoning. However, some things were bigger than any one man or god. The population of Urgu was superstitious and religious. They had proof that gods existed, and nothing could stop them from worshipping.

There were devotions to other gods, but eventually those mostly faded away or existed in the fringes, and the Church of the Six took over, amalgamating bits of every tradition to appeal to as many as possible, and staking their claim as the one of the most important forces in Urgu. It started in a little church, high atop a hill overlooking the Emerald City, where worshippers met in secret, under magic that protected them from the prying eyes of the gods they worshipped.

All that knowledge returned to me when I smelled the flowers in that field of orchid-calla lily hybrids. There were still gaps in my memory, and I could feel the locks pressing on parts of my brain, but a great flood rushed upon me and gave me the ability to continue my quest.

The church was a relic of the past. There was not even stained glass in the windows. They hadn't had money for that. It was a small, humble building, built by the hands of the first worshippers of the church, who became the first apostles, who went out and spread the doctrine.

Still, pieces of the modern churches could still be seen in its ancient architecture. The white steeple, for instance, that rose, chipped, from the small structure, became a standard. There were grooved holes where gems would have sat, just like on the newer buildings, but they had been stolen over the years. Paintings of the Six smiled down from the ceiling. They would have been magnificent in their prime, but they were faded and damaged with the passage of time.

A pity, I thought as I walked towards the lectern next to a wooden altar. On the top of it, a crude wooden carving of the Six sat dusty, gazing out on the empty, broken pews. Somehow, I knew exactly what to do, as if a divine force was guiding my actions. I knelt under the altar and felt the dais for a loose board or something else to show me the path. "*Ipsum revelare.*"

I waved my hand over the floor and a small carved flower appeared in it. Instinctively, I pressed my hand on it, and it revealed a small, golden lock, perfect for the key. It popped open when I inserted the key into the lock, and the sound of gears came from behind me. I spun on my heels to see the floor slide away, uncovering stairs that led into the darkness below.

I pulled the key from the lock and stepped down the stairs. "*Lux.*"

A small light filled my hands and lit my way. The walls

were black obsidian and damp. The stairs felt holy, sacred even, and it looked as though nobody had descended them in hundreds of years. At the bottom, I continued through a tight hallway. Along the halls, etched into the cracked stone, were epitaphs of two snakes entwined together, the symbol for my mother's house. I ran my hands against them to feel a bit of her inside of me. The stone was cool to the touch, but I still felt warm being close to her.

The hallway emptied me into a small room with a small, gilded chest in the middle of it, propped up on a stone pedestal so that it was level with my hips when I walked up to it.

"Here goes nothing."

I placed my key into the lock, and it gave, flipping open to divulge its secrets. I peered inside to discover my boon, only to have my heart drop and my stomach sink.

The chest was empty.

CHAPTER 55
CHELLE

"What is this place?" We passed through the small alleys into the main street of a town that, with every step we took, passed into a new era, from medieval to renaissance to steampunk to modern.

"The Celestial Realm," Rose said. "It's an anachronistic nightmare."

"I hate it." I trudged along until I was even with Rose. Behind us, Nox loomed large. Rose pulled Hypnos's sunglasses from her pocket, and we used them to hide Nox's eyes. "Seriously."

"It's definitely not ideal," she replied. "But there's no way for us to get home without some help, and pretty soon every god at Zeus's command is going to be after us."

"I don't know if he's the leader of the Board. He seemed kind of weak to me."

Rose yanked me down another alley. "I watched him pull Nox's soul out of her body and stuff it in a box. There is nothing weak about him."

"Fair enough." I looked around. "Are you sure you're taking us somewhere safe?"

She shrugged. "As sure as I can be about anything when it comes to the gods." The road dead-ended at a door with a metal gorgon knocker on it. "I'm sorry about this. It wasn't my idea."

"It's fine. Why shouldn't we be servants to the gods here, too?"

Rose struck the door with the knocker and the metal gorgon came to life, cracking its jaw and nearly losing the metal ring in her mouth. "What do you wa—" The gorgon caught my eye. "Oh, hello love. I haven't seen one of my own kind in a long time. Aren't you lovely?"

I smiled. "Thank you. After the day I've had, it's nice to hear a compliment."

"We need to get inside," Rose said. "Please."

"What is the password?"

Rose furrowed her brow and thought for a moment, before snapping her fingers in frustration. "Shoot, I don't remember it. Isn't there anything else we can do to get inside? It's really important."

"Maybe there's something we can do." The gorgon looked from Rose to me. "Let me see a demonstration of your powers, little one."

"Really?" I smiled. "If you insist."

I reached up and pulled the glasses off Nox's eyes, showing off the orange glow to them and making the knocker howl with laughter. "Oh, that's rich. I haven't seen a gorgon overpower a god's will in a long time. You must be pretty powerful."

"There's a price on my head. Both of ours, really." I squeezed Rose's hand. "Which is why we would really appreciate getting inside somewhere safe."

The knocker's face grew long. "Well, I'm not sure how

safe it is in there, but for you, dear, I'll let you in, especially since I remember your friend."

"Then why didn't you let me in before?" Rose balled her hands into fists.

"Nothing personal." The door clicked open. "It's just my job."

We continued down the hallway until we reached a bar filled with wooden chairs. Three people sat around a table in the center. When we entered, they turned, and I realized they weren't people at all; they were gods.

"Oh thank the realms!" One of the women rushed over to Rose. "We lost contact with you and thought the worst." She turned to me. "Is this her?"

"It is." Rose nodded. "Hepit, Chelle. Chelle, Hepit."

"It's nice to meet you," I said with a tilt of my head.

"And I see you brought us a gift." A tall, slender, dark-skinned man in a nice suit rose from the table to study Nox, then looked around. "What happened to Hypnos?"

Rose held out her hands. "We lost him in the fray, Rama. I'm sorry."

Hepit scrunched up her face in concern. "Not the best news, but it looks like you captured the prize. How are you, Nox? Happy to be out of prison?"

I stepped between them. "She's...not herself. Zeus got to her. I had to—"

Another woman walked over, eyeing Nox with curiosity. "Are you mind-controlling her?"

"That's right."

"It was quick thinking by Chelle," Rose said. "Nox was about to kill us."

Rama bit his lip. "It's an undignified way to live, but at least you brought her body with you. That will be useful before the end."

"And where is Red, Adita?" Rose asked.

The final woman in the room cleared her throat. "With the new—with Nox being gone, we needed somebody inside the prison to pull her back. Gabrielle agreed to be our 'man on the inside,' as it were."

"You let her get captured!" I shouted. "How could you?"

Rama held up his hands. "Whoa, we're not the bad guys. You two escaped, and that's great, but the Board will never stop until they capture you. The only way to get any peace is by ending their reign of terror, and the only way to do that is by reuniting Nox's soul with her body. That means we need Red inside the prison. I don't like it any more than you, but she's safe, for now. I still have my connection to her and will make sure nothing happens to her."

"You've already failed at that," Rose grumbled.

"Be that as it may," Adita said. "You don't have much other choice but to trust us, unless you want to take your chances on your own."

I sighed. She was right. "Do you at least have a plan?"

Hepit nodded. "The beginnings of one, but we need a little more time to lay out the details. Why don't you go upstairs to rest, and we'll come for you soon?"

"I'm not tired," Rose said.

"That's the adrenaline," Rama said. "It will fade soon, and then you will crash, hard. Better to get in front of it. Relax. You are among friends."

"We'll see about that," I said, pulling Rose by the hand to the stairs. At least I had her. What was the worst that could happen, so long we were together?

CHAPTER 56

NIMUE

I had watched, horrified, as my skin was pulled from my body and given to Cassandra, and how I was left with the disgusting mess that was the muscles and sinew underneath. I tried my best not to look at myself as they dragged me to my cell under the castle. The guard's touch burned like fire on my skin, and as I thrashed against them my movements made them hurt even more, and the pain forced me to pass out.

When I woke up, I was in a rat-infested cage with nothing but a searing draft for company, and every time the air blew across my skin I gasped in pain. Cassandra was not wrong. Having your skin flayed from your body made every movement agony.

"Heal," I whispered, trying to get my skin to blister over, but it was no use. This was old, powerful magic. "Rust," I eked out to the door to the cell, but it would not corrode. Once again, I was powerless against the forces of the gods.

Soon, this torture would drive me as mad as the King in Yellow and Epiales combined. I chuckled at the thought that I had ever been frightened of Epiales, when he was nothing compared to King Hastur, and the pain of the thought sent a ripple down my spine.

Footsteps came down the hall, high heels on stone. Their owner stepped into view: Cassandra, wearing my skin, as if it were the most normal thing in the universe.

"What do you want?" I hissed.

She slid a tray towards me. "I brought you some food from the banquet. I tried to find the things that would least unsettle a human's stomach."

I shot a look of disgust at her. "I'm not eating that, traitor."

"I'm sorry. You have no—no idea what it is like to live in constant pain, every second of every day; to be excommunicated from everything you've ever known."

"Actually," I said, "I do."

"Of course." She nodded. "He offered me clemency if I funneled information to him. If I brought him Rapunzel's new pet. That was what he told me." She knelt down. "That's who he wants, Nimue. He wanted the Faceless Woman. He wants her stripped low and destroyed, until she begs for a death that will never come."

"Why is he so obsessed with her?"

"She is the only being on this planet that can rival his power, and he knows it." She knelt closer. "Even Baba can't do that. You can use that. Pledge loyalty to him. Become his consort. Bide your time."

Her neck was close enough, so I lunged for it, digging my nails into my own beautiful skin, which showed the universe in it and had made me feel more powerful than I ever had before. "Why shouldn't I kill you now, traitor?"

"I am still—I am still on your side. I just—need more time to help you."

She was lying, clearly, but I didn't know why, except to live another second. I decided it wasn't worth it to kill her. Guilt might be a good motivator.

"You still want King Hastur dead?"

She choked for breath. "More than anything. We all do, but we fear the Faceless Woman, and Baba as well. At least with King Hastur, our suffering is known."

"What you need is freedom from all tyranny, Cassandra." I released her from my grasp, and she rubbed at her neck.

"I know. And I believe you can deliver it to us. Gather the princesses to your cause, gain King Hastur's confidence, and you take the crown for yourself."

"And become Baba's puppet?"

She shook her head. "There is a way out of even her magic. I will show you. I promise."

"You expect me to become queen of this horrible realm?" I scoffed. "I would rather die."

She stood. "Well, that can be arranged. Meanwhile, you'll have time to think about it as the wind whips through you. Be glad he doesn't send you to the wolves, like he did for me. It was only divine mercy that allowed me to live through that and build a life for myself." She continued up the stairs towards the party still raging above, turning back to say, "You will have to rely on the kindness of monsters before the end or be eaten by them."

I watched until she disappeared from view. She made a compelling case. Queen of the Dark Planet was quite a bit better than being flayed and stuck in a dungeon. I would deal with Cassandra at the appropriate time, but until then, she might be a powerful ally. Still, the thought of flaying her inch by inch brought a smile to my face as my head fell against the cold stone, and I braced myself for a night of torture from the unforgiving wind.

I had been laid low before and risen from the ashes. I would rise once again, and strike fear in all those that stood against me.

AUTHOR'S NOTE

It's really interesting coming back to a story for a third arc and trying to make everything both familiar and unsettling at the same time. I always knew that the third arc would take place in the Celestial Realm, but the Faceless Woman only came about when I found the perfect cover for this series, which was equal parts creepy and majestic.

After nearly destroying the Fairy Realm and Earth in the last books, I knew that Nimue would need to be brought down in this one. In the original outline, Nimue did kill King Hastur, but as I wrote her part of the story, I found myself wanting to get to know the princesses better, and if I continued my original path then they would be relegated to the background. In other words, King Hastur survived because I love writing gothic princesses.

Nimue's story has always been the darkest, going all the way back to when she reached the Nightmare Realm at the end of book two, and this one took it up several notches. I've been wanting to introduce my love of Lovecraft's mythos into this universe for a while, and while I did some of that in the first arc, with Etsop, I really wanted to lean into it with the Dark Planet.

As for the Rose/Chelle storyline...can't they just be happy? No, because then where would the story be?

So, I have another confession. When I had Nox say "I thought I had more time" at the end of *The Sunken Kingdom*, I just really wanted a cool cliffhanger. I didn't quite know what would happen with her, or that she was the lynchpin to the Board's plans. In fact, I had to go back once I came up with the idea and revise the eighth book again so that it made sense with the new direction.

With Red chasing Nimue, I needed something to get her into the main storyline, and not just make it a revenge plot. Rama was originally supposed to be a one scene character, but I needed somebody to play off of Red. In the outline she was on a quest to find a key to open the door to the Dark Planet, but I cut that when I found a way to bring her into the Celestial Realm and save Chelle.

That scene with Red and Rose is one of my favorites in the whole book, and the whole series. When two friends get together, after thinking they will never see each other again...it's just the best.

The cover I bought for the Faceless Woman made me so confused when I first took possession of it, which begs the question...why did I buy it?

I wish I had a better answer, but it was just one of those things. I knew I had to have it, though I didn't know why or how it would work in the Obsidian Spindle Saga. When I went about figuring her character out, the only way I could justify her condition was that her face was removed for defying the gods. That premise allowed me to bring in the Dream Realm and introduce Ariel to the mix. Ariel was easily the hardest character to introduce into the narrative.

She was there because I had a cover for the Drowned Princess, and because I love a good challenge. She was supposed to be integral to the plot of the last arc, but then... she wasn't.

Luckily, it all worked out and I was able to find a way to bring her into the narrative while reintroducing the Dream Realm, which is still my favorite of all the realms we've visited in the series, and the one I spent the most time creating.

The good news about Ariel is that I've been dropping hints about her for many books now, all the way back to the first arc when they first talked about the Drowned Princess. That's how long I've had this Drowned Princess cover. I've literally been sitting on it since the very beginning of writing this series.

Speaking of...the next book of this series is called *The Drowned Princess,* and it sees Ariel looking for the left and right eyes of the Faceless Woman, and we learn more about how Rapunzel came to anger the gods.

I hope you'll join me in *The Drowned Princess,* book 10 of the Obsidian Spindle Saga.

THE DROWNED PRINCESS PREVIEW

BOOK 10 OF THE OBSIDIAN SPINDLE SAGA

By:
Russell Nohelty

Edited by:
Leah Lederman

Proofread by:
Katrina Roets

Cover by:
JV Arts

Formatting by:
Turbo Kitten Industries

ROSE

I slept like a baby, which was to say I tossed and turned, waking in fits and starts, cranky and desperate to be held. We had been living in Hepit's bar for the better part of two weeks, and while I was happy to have Chelle back, I really wanted our bed, not the lumpy, hard thing that Rama had given us.

I slid out of the covers and set my feet on the cold wooden floor. The sun never shone on the Celestial Realm. iNyanga told me it was because the stars circled it, and not the other way around. The center of the universe had its beauty, sure, but I missed the warmth of a star shining on my face. There wasn't even a moon to brighten the sky, so the whole planet was the type of chilly that bristled the bones, though it stopped short of freezing.

I stepped over to the window that looked out on the anachronistic realm, with huge skyscrapers built next to ancient pagodas and thatched roof homes. The gods had lived through every time period a hundred times over on thousands of worlds, and they brought their favorite eras to their homes and those places they frequented. The bar that acted as both our salvation and our prison would have been perfectly at home in a Shakespearean play, with the banners of earls' houses hanging off the wooden balconies.

We hadn't left the pub since I'd helped Rama and his friends save Chelle and Nox from the Crystal Keep. Perhaps it was too harsh to call this pub a prison, at least compared to the Keep, but I still felt like the gods trying to endear themselves to us were more jailers than friends.

Chelle wanted to leave and take our chances back on Earth, but I was reluctant. Although we'd managed to save her in the daring escape, we left Gabrielle behind in the Crystal Keep. I didn't trust Rama and the others to rescue her without us, even though they swore to us it was as important to them as saving Nox's soul and reuniting it with the husk of her body that remained.

It was unsettling to run into Nox these days, with that vacant expression of hers. She was, more than any god I had ever known, full of confidence and will. Now, without her soul, she was more like a computer on power-save mode, staring blankly into the middle distance, and returning any question with monotone, uninspired responses.

Still, it was better having her on our side than as a puppet for Zeus and the Board that was hunting us. I didn't buy everything Rama said, but that much I believed. We had humiliated them by absconding with their prizes, and they would stop at nothing to track us down.

Patient as I was, I had grown tired of sitting on my hands. Every day we asked the Circle of Truth—the gods that resisted the Board's influence, which included Rama, Hepit, iNyanga, Aditi, and others who were only spoken about in vague whispers—whether they had finished their plotting. Always, we were told that it would just be a couple more days. I was starting to get the distinct impression they were as lost as we were and so I didn't love the thought of relying on them for our next move.

"Are you okay?" Chelle moaned as she turned over in bed. "Why are you staring out a window at half past the gods know when?"

"I think it's morning," I said. "My body says it's morning, at least."

She held out her arms. "Well, my body says it's the middle of the night, so come back to bed."

I wasn't tired, not even a little bit, but I had learned over the last few years to cherish every moment with Chelle because I didn't know how many more I would have before we were pulled apart again. She didn't like that kind of talk, but I knew it was only a matter of time.

I crawled back into bed and Chelle wrapped her arms around me. "That's better, isn't it?"

"It's very nice," I said, laying my arm around her shoulder and allowing her to nuzzle into my neck. "I love you."

She adjusted her head, and Albie snuggled on my chest along with his snake brothers and sisters that lived on Chelle's head. I pet each one of them in kind, and it made me miss my dog Cheyenne terribly. I had left her on Earth with Jamil, our wood nymph friend, thinking I would be back soon enough. I suppose I also understood that I might never be back at all. With Chelle in my arms again, I wanted nothing more than for our dog to snuggle up with the rest of the family.

"I love you, too," Chelle said with a yawn. "I know you're antsy about saving Red, but this is the most time we have spent together in, like, ever. No jobs, no school, no walking the dog, even. Am I a bad person that I kind of enjoy it?"

"No," I replied with a small smile. "There are plenty of reasons you're a bad person, but that's not one of them."

"Smart ass." She yawned again. "Your heart is beating really fast right now."

"It always does that when I'm around you," I said, kissing the top of her head.

"Corny," she mumbled. "I love it."

"I love it, too, but I have to admit, I keep waiting for the other shoe to drop."

"Maybe it won't."

"We're on the run from the gods. The other shoe will absolutely drop."

As if on cue, an explosion rocked the building and the floorboards groaned. We launched ourselves off the bed before the wood snapped and our bed crashed into a table on the floor below.

"Well, that could have been worse," I said, looking over the chasm at Chelle.

"I think it's about to," she replied. "The quiet was nice while it lasted."

RED

Turned out that jail was just as bad in the Celestial Realm as anywhere else I had been imprisoned. Once the cells were locked down, they paraded me through the cells, bloodied and bruised, as a symbol of what happened when you defied the Board. It didn't have quite the reaction they expected, though, as my every step was met with hollers and cheers that made me smile even though the pain.

After that, I was thrown in solitary confinement, with little more than rotten scraps to eat and stale water to drink. I hadn't seen the outside of the cell since they threw me in. Being confined to a prison cell without anyone to talk to wasn't much of a punishment, as I was used to being on my own for days, months at a time. In some ways, it was a blessing.

Besides, I wasn't really alone. I still had my connection with Rama that we'd used to communicate to each other. I had been beaten within inches of my life, prodded and probed, but none of that severed the connection. For the first few days I stayed frosty, given that his plan had sent me to jail. But it had also rescued Chelle and kept Rose safe

—barely—and I was more than happy to trade my freedom for theirs.

"I'm thinking of a number," Rama said.

"Is it seven?" I asked.

He liked playing games with me, at least when he wasn't busy trying to make a plan to save me from my fate. He must have felt sorry for me. I could have done two weeks of solitude standing on my head, but it was nice to have company, even if it was with a god I only half-trusted.

"Higher or lower?"

"Lower," he grumbled.

"So you had literally every other number to deal with, up to and including infinity, and you chose one of the seven numbers that were lower?"

"Six numbers."

"Zero, one, two, three, four, five, six, is seven numbers."

"Zero isn't a number."

"What?" I chuckled. "Then what is it?"

"It's the lack of a number. It's an anti-number."

"What about negative numbers?" I asked. "They're a thing, and zero is right there between one and negative one."

"I don't give much credence to negativity, dear. You should know that by now."

"Is ten a number?" I asked.

"Yes, of course."

"How, when it has zero in it? Or a hundred, or a thousand? Your argument makes no sense."

"Okay," Rama said. "Show me zero of something."

I leaned back on the crystal wall. "I can't show you, because I'm in a cell and you're not."

He sighed. "You're right. I'm sorry. It was just a turn of phrase, a bad one, mind you, but I meant no offense by it."

I slid down to the floor. "How are you coming with my escape plan?"

"Not—not well, I'm afraid."

Rama stammered, something he never did, which showed how dire the situation really was. I had kept myself in high spirits, knowing that if Rama could break Chelle and Nox out of the Crystal Keep, he could do the same for me. That hope had faded with the words he'd just spoken.

"I have faith in you," I said, even though it wasn't true.

"You shouldn't," he replied. "Nox and Chelle were a special case. They were brought to trial before the Board, giving us a window to act. You are under lock and key, with guards watching every minute of every day. Until they move you out of solitary and ease up their watch of you, we are at an impasse."

"Then I have to figure out a way out of this by myself."

"You're not alone, here. We just have to wait for a little while. Just sit tight. We will get you out of there."

I was tired of sitting tight and waiting. Luckily, escaping prisons and making the best of a bad situation were well within my skill set. I wasn't much use in the real world, where people lived in holly-hobby homes and had menial jobs, but in whatever reality I lived in, my special skills had saved my bacon more than I cared to admit.

I groaned. "Is your number three?"

There was no answer. I repeated myself a few times, then called his name. In two weeks of talking with Rama, he had never gone radio silent on me.

"Hello?" I said. "Rama? Is everything all right?"

"Holy—" he said, then I heard an explosion erupt close enough that it stung my ears even miles away. "We're under attack!"

Attack? My first thought turned to Zeus and the Board

having found him, which meant they found Rose and Chelle, too, since he was providing protection to them...and I wasn't there. I was stuck in a stupid cell, helpless.

"Are my friends, all right?" I shouted, getting to my feet and pacing the cell, desperate to get out. "Rama! Answer me!"

It was no use.

I slammed myself against the door, but it was made of solid crystal, which meant my banging did nothing but hurt. I landed with a thud on the floor. *No, no, no, no, no.* I had risked everything for Rose and was willing to give my life for her, but now I was useless, stuck in a cell while my friends were under attack.

For the first time since being brought to solitary, I felt tortured by the silence, and my own ineptitude. I hated it.

ARIEL

"What do you mean the box was empty?" Queen Aine said from her throne in the Emerald Castle. I'd been dreading this conversation since the moment I found the box hidden under the chapel in the first Church of the Six. It was supposed to contain Rapunzel's eye.

"Exactly what I said, ma'am." I breathed in deeply and puffed out my chest. "The box was resting on a pedestal in the center of the room, but it was empty."

I had searched for the left eye of Rapunzel throughout all of Oz and tracked it to the small forest shrine using clues that my mother's spirit had given me. Or perhaps it was not her spirit, but a construction made by Nox to guide me on my way. It had been hard to know which was the truth, but the moment I opened the box, the visions ceased, which told me that I had found the place Nox believed the left eye resided. Except it had been stolen from its resting place.

Queen Aine waved me closer. "Bring the box here. Maybe you are doing it wrong."

I gripped the gilded box tighter. "I know how to open a box."

"Obviously not," she growled at me. "Otherwise, we would have the eye."

I walked up the slick, emerald stairs to her throne and set the box down. Since Queen Aine was a fairy, it was nearly as big as she was, and could have kept her entombed if I simply pushed her inside.

Aine leaned into the box and felt around. "Sometimes there's a secret lever that—"

"I tried that," I said, even though as a queen she could dust me into oblivion in an instant for cutting her off. "It didn't work."

"Well, you have fat fingers. Mine are much smaller and maybe they—crap. There's no secret switch." She slid into the box and leaned her head on the wooden wall. "This is not good."

"I think that's an understatement."

The two Fates, Clotho and Lachesis, said that without the eye, the Dream Realm would fall into chaos. This theft of the eye filled my stomach with a dread so heavy I thought it might drag me to the ground.

"This is no time to despair." Queen Aine fluttered upwards. I didn't know if her words were meant for me or herself, but by the time she rose to my eye level, her face was stern and confident. "I need to see the room."

"It's about two days' ride from here, but I'm sure with your carriages we can make it sooner."

She scoffed. "I don't ride in carriages. Come closer and lean your forehead to me." I did as she asked, and she placed her tiny hands on my scalp. "Good. Now close your eyes and imagine where you found this box. Make it as real as you can in your mind."

I squeezed my eyes shut and remembered the snakes etched into the grooved walls and the cobblestone floor of the old basement. I turned the corner and rebuilt the pedestal where I found the box. After a minute or so, I had a good picture of it in my mind.

"Good, good," she said. "I see it, too."

My feet felt like they fell out from under me, and then I was plunging into a grand abyss. An instant later, I landed again on the ground, my legs shaky enough that I knelt down, stabilizing myself with my hands. We were in the basement of the church.

"There is dark magic here." Queen Aine floated ahead of me through the corridors, toward the pedestal. "I thought I smelled it on the box, but it was faint. Here, its musk is strong. The last time I felt magic this strong was...the Battle for the Heart of Urgu. Epiales's forces reeked of it; Agrona most of all."

"How could she have found this place? Nobody but Nox and myself knew, and it was locked so deep in my brain that I had no idea I even knew about it."

Queen Aine ran her hands along all the walls until she reached a dark gray stone. "Nox is careful, that much is true, but secrets have a way of getting out no matter how guarded you are. They can be unearthed for the right price and with enough time. Or with the right magic."

"So you think Agrona found the eye, then?"

"I don't know, but there was one thing the gods had while they were imprisoned in Urgu, and that's time. I wouldn't put past one of them to have found Nox's secret."

"But...Agrona died in the battle, did she not?"

Queen Aine bowed her head. "Yes. That is why we must talk to the Fates. I have the inklings of a plan, but it is foggy, and I need them to help clarify it."

ALSO BY RUSSELL NOHELTY

The Obsidian Spindle Saga

The Godsverse Chronicles

Ichabod Jones: Monster Hunter

Cthulhu is Hard to Spell

My Father Didn't Kill Himself

Sorry for Existing

Gumshoes: The Case of Madison's Father

The Invasion Saga

The Vessel

Worst Thing in the Universe

The Void Calls Us Home

The Marked Ones

The Little Bird and the Little Worm

Gherkin Boy

Find a complete list at

https://www.russellnohelty.com/books/

About the Author

Russell Nohelty is a USA Today bestselling author, publisher, and speaker. He is the author of dozens of novels and graphic novels including The Godsverse Chronicles, The Obsidian Spindle Saga, and Ichabad Jones: Monster Hunter. He has a very entertaining newsletter, which you can join at www.russellnohelty.com. He lives in Los Angeles with his wife and dogs.

Get one of my favorite books for free at:
    www.russellnohelty.com/mail
    Substack:
    https://authorstack.substack.com
    Bookbub:
    https://www.bookbub.com/profile/russell-nohelty